Slaphead Chame

Also by Jerry Raine

SMALLTIME
FRANKIE BOSSER COMES HOME

Slaphead Chameleon

Jerry Raine

VICTOR GOLLANCZ
LONDON

The right of Jerry Raine to be identified as the author of this work has been asserted by him in accordance with the Copyright, Designs and Patents Act, 1988.

First published in Great Britain in 2000 by Victor Gollancz
An imprint of Orion Books Ltd
Orion House, 5 Upper St Martin's Lane,
London WC2H 9EA

A CIP catalogue record for this book is available
from the British Library

Typeset at The Spartan Press Ltd,
Lymington, Hants

Printed and bound in Great Britain by
Clays Ltd, St Ives plc

Special thanks to Jim Driver and Paul Charles for getting the show on the road. To Pam Smith for her endless enthusiasm and positive thinking. To Sabrina Pillay, a wonderful three-year-old. And to Kris Kristofferson for a lifetime of inspiration.

For my parents Margaret and Peter Raine,
and for my brother Nic.

1

The day Jason Campbell bought his first pair of cowboy boots was the day his life changed for ever. He was walking past a shoe shop in Woodvale High Street when he saw them from the corner of his eye and was smitten; they were dark brown and ankle-length with a small gold buckle on the side, with a price tag that said ninety-eight pounds.

Jason had never worn a pair of cowboy boots before, and thought they might be a talisman to change the bad luck he was having with his fading singing career. So, checking he had his credit card with him, he stepped inside to try them on.

Five hours later, wearing his fantastic new purchase, Jason stepped on stage at the Mojo Club in central London wondering if anyone had noticed them. He plugged in his black Takamine guitar, adjusted the microphone stand and proceeded to sing his usual set.

He sang for thirty minutes, six songs, and talked a little about them in between. For once the Mojo audience actually seemed to be listening, and when he walked off stage to generous applause, Jason thought, Yes! this is what it's all about. He walked back through the bar with his guitar, and up to the offices where he'd left his case.

He had just finished putting his things together when he heard footsteps coming up the stairs. He turned and saw a middle-aged man walking towards him with a smile on his face. He was about five-nine, slightly overweight, wearing a baseball cap. He had a light-coloured moustache and stubble over the rest of his face. He walked over to Jason and said, 'Excellent set. Can I buy you a drink?'

Jason shook the offered hand.

'My name's Charles Penn,' the man said, with a soft Irish accent. 'I work for the Reivers Agency.'

Jason had never heard of them but presumed they were something in the music business. He felt his heart beat a little faster. He left his things in the office and followed Penn downstairs.

'What would you like?' Penn asked when they were at the bar.

'A dry white wine would be good,' Jason said. He looked across the bar and saw the owner of the Mojo smiling at him, giving him the thumbs-up.

Penn led Jason away, into the alley by the front door. 'Always too crowded,' he said. 'I don't know how anyone plays there.'

'It's got a good atmosphere,' Jason said. 'I keep coming back for more.'

'How much do they pay you?' Penn asked.

'Twenty pounds for half an hour.'

'Is this all you do?'

Jason laughed. 'No. I'm a guitar teacher really. I live in Woodvale in Surrey. I just do this to get me out of the house and supplement my income.'

'Well, you've got some great songs.'

'Thanks.'

'Have you heard of a country singer called Calista Shaw?'

Jason shook his head. 'Can't say I have.'

'She comes from Texas but made it big in Nashville three years ago. She's done two albums, both of them big sellers. Well, I'm her UK agent. She's touring here next week, but the support act she was bringing over has been taken ill. She wants me to find someone else. How would you like the job?'

'You're joking!' Jason said, not believing what he was hearing.

'Not at all. How would you like to be a support act on a tour? Eighteen dates in all, covering England, Scotland, Ireland and Wales. You don't have to do the Irish ones if you don't want to. If you drop out of those it'll be twelve for you. You'll get a hundred pounds per show. You'll have to pay your own expenses.'

Jason sipped his wine. 'I don't sing country songs, though.'

'They're country-ish, and they're good. That's all that matters. A good song will hold its own anywhere.'

'When does this start?'

'On Saturday. Not much notice, I'm afraid. Here, let me give you my card and a tour listing. Think about it for a day, then give me a ring. I need to know tomorrow, though.'

Jason took the card and a piece of paper Penn handed him.

'I've got to go,' Penn said. 'I've got another show to catch. Give me a ring.'

'OK,' Jason nodded, and once again shook Penn's hand.

He watched the music agent put his wineglass back into the Mojo and then walk away down the alley. When he was about halfway down he turned and said, 'I like the boots, by the way. Cool.'

As he drove back to Woodvale, Jason could barely contain his thoughts. He knew he would ring Charles Penn tomorrow and accept the tour, excluding the Irish dates. That would mean twelve hundred pounds for him, less expenses, but he wouldn't tell the taxman about it. He wouldn't clear much in the end, but it would be a great experience. He would have to cancel his lessons for the three weeks or so he'd be away, but that would be no problem. Maybe this would be the launch pad that his singing career had always needed. Maybe it was time for all the low-key gigs over the years to finally pay off.

He had read the tour listing after Charles Penn had disappeared, and although it was a daunting schedule it would be a lot easier without any Irish dates. Jason had the urge to tell someone about it, and couldn't wait until he got back to his house. He hoped one of his lodgers was still up so he could tell them. He looked at his watch. It was still only ten-thirty.

Jason had taken lodgers into his three-bedroom house during the last two years to help pay his large mortgage. He had bought the semi-detached with his old girlfriend Heather, but when they'd split up Jason had taken on the responsibility alone, and eventually bought out Heather's half. Sometimes he wished he had just sold the house back in 1995, but he supposed it was an investment and somewhere he could always call home. After a bad experience with his first lodger, things had run relatively smoothly since, and his present two were the best he'd had so far. One was a trainee supervisor at the local swimming pool called Dave, and the other was an antiques dealer called Geoff. They all got on well together and Jason almost felt guilty taking the rent from them every month, a handy five hundred pounds between them.

An hour later Jason pulled his blue Nissan into his front drive and took his guitar case from the back seat. He was glad to see that the living-room lights were on, so someone was at home, probably Dave.

Pushing open the front door, Jason left his guitar in the hallway and walked into the living room. Dave was sitting on the sofa watching TV; he always had it on, even when he wasn't watching it.

'How did it go?' Dave asked, a friendly smile on his face.

'Great,' Jason said. 'And you'll never believe this, but I got spotted by a hotshot music agent. I'm going on a nationwide tour!'

'You're bullshitting me,' Dave said.

'I'm not. This bloke came up to me after the show and

offered me twelve dates with an American country singer. Starting on Saturday. Here, I've got his card.'

Jason reached in his jacket and pulled out the card Penn had given him. He watched as Dave read it. 'The Reivers Agency. Never heard of them.'

'Neither have I, but who gives a shit? This is the break I've been waiting for!' Jason clenched his fist and punched the air.

Dave laughed. 'This must be worth a drink. Have a beer on me!' He disappeared to the kitchen and came back with two cans of Heineken Export. They popped them open, toasted success and took a swig each.

They sat on the sofa while Jason showed Dave his tour listing. The first four dates were in Glasgow, Aberdeen, South Shields and Preston, and then Calista Shaw would be going to Northern Ireland for three dates on her own. Jason would then pick up the tour in London on 5 October, and follow it with concerts in Cardiff, Portsmouth and Wavendon, wherever the hell that was.

'It's near Milton Keynes,' Dave told him.

Then there was another spell in Ireland for Calista, this one down South, and Jason would rejoin her in Norwich on 14 October, followed by Cambridge, Coventry and Leeds, where it would all end on 17 October.

'It's a busy schedule,' Dave said. 'You'll be sick of trains by the end of it.'

'I'll be riding on a high,' Jason said. 'Hopefully.'

They finished their beers and Dave went to the kitchen for more.

Jason tried to relax, but his stomach was still churning. He wondered if he'd get on with Calista Shaw. Maybe they'd become good buddies and she'd invite him to Nashville to cut an album. The possibilities were endless.

Dave returned with the new cans and had just sat down on the sofa when the bay window behind them exploded. They both jumped up in fright and Dave dropped his beer on the floor.

They looked at each other.

'What the fuck was that?' Dave asked.

'Someone just threw something through the window,' Jason said, stating the obvious. He was frozen to the spot and experiencing a fear he hadn't felt since 1995. He looked at Dave's beer oozing on to the carpet.

'I'll go and see who it was,' Dave said, and quickly left the room.

Jason put his beer down and picked up Dave's can. He pulled the sofa away from the window and pulled back the curtain. Lying there on the floor amid the broken glass was half a brick.

And attached to it with a rubber band was a note.

2

On the same Monday in September, Detective Inspector Jesse Morgan of the Woodvale police force was also making life-altering decisions. The first one came at four in the afternoon when he walked into Chief Superintendent Cole's office and handed in two months' notice.

'Are you completely mad?' Cole said, from behind his large, orderly desk.

'Completely sane,' Morgan replied, and then gave Cole his official reason why. 'After twenty-two years in the force,' he told him, 'there's nothing more for me to learn, and as it looks as though I won't be promoted any higher, there's little point in me carrying on.'

For the next half-hour Cole tried to talk him out of it, but there was no way Morgan was going to change his mind.

Later in the canteen, Morgan told his close friend Detective Sergeant Ian Kiddie the more personal reason behind it.

'It's Aidan's death,' he said. 'It's really got to me. I keep wondering why it was him and not me.'

Kiddie nodded and took a sip of coffee. 'I think anyone would think that. It was a shocking accident. But just make sure you're not rushing into anything.'

Morgan shook his head. 'It's been over three weeks now. I've had time to think it through. I know I'm making the right decision.'

The accident involving Aidan Pearson had happened in an A. C. Cobra sports car. Pearson, a twenty-four-year-old, had spent six years building it from a kit his father had bought him six years previously. When the machine was finished he put a list of his days off on the staff noticeboard for anyone who wanted to take a trial spin with him. Morgan put his name down for something to do. He was the fourth policeman on the list.

It had been a dull Saturday morning when Morgan had driven up to Pearson's lodgings, and he had felt quite excited when he'd seen the metallic-blue Cobra sitting there in the drive, double white stripes going down the centre of its bonnet and boot. Pearson welcomed him with his usual smile and showed him the outstanding features of the classic car: the chromed side exhausts and air vents, and the imitation Halibrand alloy wheels. He also proudly told him that it could accelerate from nought to a hundred in nine seconds, thanks to its wonderful American V8 engine.

The Cobra was open-topped, and out on the country roads Morgan had felt quite chilly as the wind raced around his body. He had never been that interested in cars, and he had heard a few years ago how a relation of his had contracted serious arthritis at the young age of fifty, caused, so his doctor had suspected, by thirty years of driving open-topped sports cars. But Morgan didn't have the heart to tell Pearson this as he revved his way around tight, blind corners.

The fateful crash had happened some twenty minutes into their drive, when they were on a narrow country road stuck behind a coach. Pearson had pulled the Cobra to the right to overtake, but as they were passing, the Cobra's offside wheels had bumped over the grass verge and remained there. They were now tram-lining with the coach next to them, and Pearson had panicked and driven faster.

When the coach was behind them, Pearson pulled hard left on the steering wheel to free the car from the verge, but then the Cobra jumped violently and headed for the opposite bank. There was no time to straighten the vehicle up, and they went crashing over the bank and into a tree.

The whole thing had happened so quickly that Morgan

just sat in the passenger seat in stunned silence, looking at the smoke seeping from under the bonnet. Then he glanced over at Pearson and was horrified to see that a branch had gone straight into his neck and that he was on the point of passing out. Pearson was looking straight at him with an apologetic smile, while blood seeped from his wound.

Morgan quickly unclipped his four-point harness, climbed from the car and ran over to the coach, which had already stopped. One of the passengers phoned for an ambulance on his mobile, while Morgan grabbed the coach's fire extinguisher and put out the flames that were just starting under the Cobra's bonnet. Then he had a look at Pearson.

Morgan and the coach driver tried to stem the flow of blood, but the branch of the tree was lodged tight in Pearson's neck, and when the ambulance arrived ten minutes later, Pearson was already dead. He had lost consciousness after about five minutes, and Morgan hoped he hadn't suffered too much.

The ambulance took Morgan away as well. He had glass in his hair and cuts on his forehead, which he hadn't noticed at the time. At the hospital they stitched him up quickly and then sent him home, where he fell into bed in a trance.

And he had been in a trance ever since.

Although he had seen many dead bodies in his twenty-two years as a policeman, Pearson's death had got to Morgan, so he thought, because it was the first time he had actually seen someone being killed. He also felt guilty that the branch hadn't struck him instead, a man of forty-eight whose life was meandering nowhere, rather than a popular twenty-four-year-old with a rich life ahead of him. The whole thing seemed like such a waste. He thought that maybe this was a sign, some higher force telling him to get on with his life instead of wasting away in a job going nowhere. Maybe it was time he moved on to pastures new, where he could work normal hours and mix with everyday people instead of always regarding them with suspicion. He decided for definite that it was.

'Fancy a drink after work?' Morgan asked Kiddie, who was just finishing his coffee and reading a newspaper someone had left behind.

'No can do,' Kiddie said. 'I have to get home to put up some shelves.'

Morgan smiled. 'What an exciting life you lead.'

They talked a few minutes more and then Morgan went back to his office. He spent the remainder of his shift catching up on paperwork and at six o'clock jumped into his car and drove to the nearest off-licence.

Morgan's second major decision of the day was that he was going to give up drinking for good. He had been a slave to the poison for too long, and it was another complication he wanted to remove from his life. He also thought it was the cause of his mood swings of the past eight years or so.

In the off-licence, he bought a bottle of Bollinger, some Kettle chips and some cheese and dips. He was going to have a solitary celebration and then quit.

For as long as he could remember, his routine after work had always been similar to this: go home, open a bottle of wine or beer and not quit until at least six glasses or more later. Although he knew he was no alcoholic, this amount added up over a month was more than a man his age should be getting through, and as he felt he couldn't cut it down, the only way was to cut it out altogether.

Once at home, Morgan sat in front of the TV with his feast, then fell into bed at midnight with his head spinning in a pleasurable way. He savoured the feeling, knowing he would never have it again.

The next morning he had a slight hangover, but felt like a different man already. He knew it would be the last hangover he ever suffered, and that was reason enough to be content.

After a shower and breakfast, he went into his overgrown,

neglected garden, and spent most of the day mowing the lawn and trimming the hedges. He worked up a nice sweat in the September sun, and at five o'clock worked up some more sweat by going for a three-mile run. After shower number two and a quick beard trim, he settled down in front of the TV and watched an exciting European football match between Celtic and Liverpool. It finished two-all and Morgan fell into bed exhausted but satisfied. It was the first time in months that he'd gone to bed sober.

He slept soundly, and didn't awake until the telephone by his bed interrupted his dreams at seven o'clock. It was the duty sergeant, an overweight buffoon called Garnett.

'Sorry to wake you, sir,' he said, 'but we've got a stiffy on the Holmethorpe Industrial Estate. At Bell's Plastics.'

Morgan winced at the word 'stiffy' as he wiped the sleep from his eyes. Was Garnett always going to be a complete moron?

'OK,' he said. 'I'm on my way. Can you ring up Kiddie as well?'

'OK,' Garnett said, and hung up.

Morgan climbed out of bed and stretched. He didn't feel like hurrying. What was the point? A dead body wasn't going anywhere.

He padded to the shower and began his second sober day.

3

The Holmethorpe Industrial Estate was situated on the outskirts of Redgate, a sister town of Woodvale. It was home to about thirty businesses of varying obscurity, and Bell's Plastics was one of the oldest. Morgan had visited Bell's only once before, to question a local man who'd been causing his neighbours grief by playing heavy-metal music loud into the night. Knowing the case would take ages to reach a conclusion in court, Morgan had taken the man aside one day and had a stern word in his ear. The man had left the area soon after, and Morgan reckoned he had saved a lot of time and taxpayers' money.

The drive to Redgate only took five minutes, and Morgan parked his car at the front of the factory. He saw Detective Sergeant Ian Kiddie emerging from the front door of the offices with a man dressed in blue overalls.

'Glad you could make it,' Kiddie said sarcastically, as Morgan climbed from his car. 'This is Dick Frosty, the foreman of the shift. He'll take us to the body.'

Morgan nodded at the man and decided to ignore Kiddie's remark. They followed Frosty as he led them out of the car park and down the side of the factory.

'I wonder how many more of these you'll get,' Kiddie said. 'Could be the last one before you hang up your boots.'

'With any luck,' Morgan said.

They passed some sliding doors that led on to the factory floor. There was a hum of machines and several workers were staring at them. A wave of warm air hit Morgan's face and then evaporated.

'Did you see the match last night?' Kiddie asked. He was a large Scotsman with ginger hair and moustache, and had no doubt been rooting for Celtic.

Morgan nodded. 'A satisfactory result, I thought.'

'Liverpool were lucky,' Kiddie snorted. 'A last-minute equalizer.'

'I hardly think a fifty-yard run, beating three players, is a lucky equalizer. McManaman is a fine player when he gets it right.'

'Only because he's got a Celtic name,' Kiddie said.

Morgan laughed, but then had to wipe the smile off his face as they approached the backyard of the factory. There were about ten workers staring at the dead body, which lay about twenty feet away behind blue and white police tape. There were two uniformed constables with them and one of them sauntered over.

'Get these people away from here,' Morgan said forcefully, and the constable walked sheepishly away and started telling people to move. 'Don't they teach them anything at Hendon?' he said to Kiddie.

Kiddie just said, 'After you,' as he held up the tape and Morgan ducked under.

The body lay on its front in between two stacks of wooden pallets, on a concrete surface, blood all around its head, which had obviously been struck with a blunt instrument. Morgan knelt down at a safe distance and asked, 'What was his name?'

'Jim Brady,' Kiddie said. 'Fifty-five. Been at the factory eight years.'

Brady was wearing blue overalls like the rest of the workers, covered in grease and grime from the machines. His sleeves were rolled to his elbows and there was a fading tattoo on his left forearm. Morgan couldn't make out what it was. He stood up and said, 'SOCO are on their way, I presume?'

'As fast as their vehicles can carry them,' Kiddie said.

'Which isn't very fast by the look of things. Who found the body?'

Kiddie turned and pointed to a young worker who hadn't left the scene and was standing by Dick Frosty. 'That chap there. Simon Cowl is his name. Came out here for a smoke just after six.'

They ducked back under the tape and walked over to the two men. Morgan introduced himself to Cowl and said to Frosty, 'I need two spare offices for interviewing and I want no one to go home until we're through. There's no need to shut the factory down, though.'

'No problem,' Frosty said.

'Can you get some more help down here?' Morgan asked Kiddie. 'Might as well get Hickle down as well. He hasn't had a murder since he arrived. I'll interview Cowl and get the ball rolling.'

'OK,' Kiddie said, and the four of them walked back up the side of the factory, leaving the two constables on their own with the corpse.

The young lad called Simon Cowl sat opposite Jesse Morgan in one of the offices allocated to the police. The walls were full of photos of plastic objects, graphs, a supposedly tasteful glamour calendar and the usual office clutter. It was the personnel manager's office, apparently. Morgan felt honoured.

Simon Cowl was a slim young man with longish wavy hair. He was twenty-three and was only working in the factory, so he told Morgan, until something better came along. On first impressions Morgan thought him too intelligent to be working in a factory, but Cowl told him that some people actually liked working in them. You could shut off the outside world and just get on with your mundane task without having to worry about anything. It was almost a form of meditation. Morgan didn't know if he agreed with that train of thought, but didn't have time to argue about it. He changed the subject to the murder victim. 'So how did you find Jim Brady's body?' he asked.

'I sneaked out for a cigarette break,' Cowl said. 'I started at six this morning, and at a quarter past walked outside with a cup of coffee.'

'You needed a break after only fifteen minutes?'

Cowl smiled. 'There wasn't much happening on my machine. I usually last longer.'

'So you walked down to the backyard. Is that where people normally go for their breaks?'

Cowl shook his head. 'Most people have breaks on the factory floor. Or in the canteen. I like to get some fresh air, though.'

'And fill it full of smoke.'

'Exactly. Nothing like smoking in the fresh air. I often go down there. Just to get out of the noise, really.'

'And he was lying there when you arrived?'

'Yes. I didn't touch a thing. I went back inside and told Dick Frosty. And he called you.'

Morgan nodded. 'What shift was Brady on, your shift?'

'No. The night shift. He should've left at six.'

Morgan made a note on his pad. So Brady was probably killed in the middle of the night. But how would someone get him into the backyard? Or had he gone down to meet someone? 'So what was Jim Brady like?' he asked.

'Not a very nice bloke really,' Cowl said. 'He annoyed a lot of people, including me. But I wouldn't have thought anyone here would have wanted to kill him, or even hurt him as such.'

'And why didn't you like him?'

'He just didn't seem to like young people. We had a few students working here in the summer, and he used to give them a lot of stick. When they left he transferred the stick on to me. And I'm not even a student. I think he treated the older blokes all right, though.'

'What sort of stick?'

15

'Just taking the piss. But not in a joky way. There was always nastiness behind it. I think he had a chip on his shoulder. He'd been in jail as well, I think.'

Morgan's interest picked up. 'Jail? How do you know that?'

'I've heard others talking about it. One of his old jobs was as a publican. He used to drink a lot. He's also been married a few times. Put the three together, and I think you've got the reason why he was in jail. But I've never found out the whole story.'

'Well, I'm sure we'll find out. Anything else you can think of?'

Cowl thought for a moment then shook his head. 'No, that's about it.'

'OK,' Morgan said. 'We may want to talk to you again, but for now I don't want to take up any more of your time. I'm sure you can't wait to get back to your meditation.'

Cowl smiled and left the room.

Morgan stood up and stretched, then turned to look out of the window. On the opposite side of the road was a building where contact lenses were made. He supposed they had to be made somewhere. He thought back to the last murder on the Holmethorpe Industrial Estate. That had been back in the summer of 1995 on a builder's yard that had since closed down. A psycho called Gator had pushed the old man that ran it down a muddy slope to his death. It had all been part of a bad week when Gator had claimed five lives altogether; not bad going considering the average for the area was around eight a year. Morgan shuddered just thinking about it. It was a week he was never likely to forget.

There was a knock on the door and his next interviewee was standing there, a middle-aged man in greasy overalls. Morgan ushered him in. He almost felt like a personnel manager.

4

It was late afternoon by the time Jesse Morgan got back to Woodvale police station. He had left Ian Kiddie at Bell's factory and Detective Inspector Bill Hickle was also helping out. Nothing of much interest had turned up yet, but Morgan was keen to look into Brady's prison record.

Pushing open the swing doors at the front of the building, Morgan saw a man sitting in reception who he recognized. He was in his late thirties or early forties with longish dark hair, and wore glasses. He was sitting on his hands and tapping his feet, looking worried and nervous. Morgan nodded at him but didn't get any response as he made his way through the security lock to the offices. It was only when he was back behind his desk that he realized who the man was. He stood up and went back down to reception. The man was still there.

Morgan went up to him and said, 'I thought I recognized you. Weren't you mixed up in that awful Gator business a few years ago? I was only thinking about him earlier this morning.'

The man looked up at Morgan and nodded. 'How could I forget Gator? But I don't remember you.'

'Detective Inspector Morgan. I interviewed you at the time.' Morgan sat down next to him. 'How's the thumb? Gator broke it, if I remember correctly.'

He watched the man look down at his right thumb and move it. 'It's OK now. It took over six months before I could play the guitar again, though.'

Morgan looked at him, more pieces of the story coming

back now. The man was a guitar teacher in Woodvale. 'What's your name again?' he asked.

'Jason Campbell.'

'Jason Campbell, that's right. You rented a room in your house to Karl Spoiler, and then Phil Gator came on the scene. Then all hell broke loose.'

'A nightmare.'

Morgan watched as Campbell visibly shivered. It was probably something Campbell didn't like talking about. 'So what brings you here?' he asked. 'Failing to pay your car tax?'

Campbell gave him a rueful smile. 'If only. It's slightly more serious than that. I think the ghost of Gator is about to rise again.'

'Pardon me?'

Campbell looked uneasily at the other people in reception. 'Can we talk in private somewhere?' he asked.

Jason Campbell had never been in a Detective Inspector's office before, but it looked like any other office to him except for the crime posters on the walls: there were filing cabinets, a fresh-water machine and a wooden desk full of paper, which Detective Inspector Morgan sat behind.

He remembered Morgan now. He had given Jason a hard time in one of the interview rooms after the Gator case, and Jason suspected he hadn't believed a word of his story, which was spot on, because Jason had made most of it up to protect his friend Frankie Bosser. Morgan looked older than Jason remembered, his beard flecked with more grey, but he was a tall, good-looking man just the same, like some kind of Gary Cooper cowboy type.

'I came here to follow something up that happened on Monday evening,' Jason said. 'I had a brick thrown through my front window with a note attached. The note said, "It's time fuck-face was caught".'

'Charming,' Morgan said.

'That's what I thought. At the time I hoped they had the

wrong house, but I reported it anyway. Then today I had another note passed through my letterbox. It came in a blank envelope.'

Jason reached in his pocket and pulled out a folded piece of paper. He laid it on the desk in front of Morgan and watched while he read. When Jason had read it, the hairs on the back of his neck had stood up, and it seemed to have the same effect on Morgan. He watched him sit up straighter in his chair.

'I'm glad I recognized you in reception,' Morgan said. 'Who was dealing with your smashed window?'

'It was a woman,' Jason said. 'Tall, slim. Good-looking, with short dark hair.'

'That'll be Beech,' Morgan said. 'Were you waiting for her just now?'

'I was waiting for anyone. There didn't seem to be anyone around.'

'We just had a murder in Redgate.'

Jason didn't know what to say about that, so he watched while Morgan sat and thought. Then he said, 'The awkward thing is, I'm about to go on a music tour on Saturday. I'll be away, on and off, for three weeks or so, and I'm worried about the two lodgers in my house. What if this nutter thinks one of them is me? The wrong person could get hurt.'

'So you'd rather it was you who got hurt?'

'No. But it's an awkward situation.'

Morgan nodded. 'But the nutter might come after you on your tour. He might start following you around. Had you thought of that?'

'No. But I don't see why he would. He doesn't know what I look like.'

'As far as you know.'

'As far as I know.' Jason hadn't thought of that. But how could the nutter know what he looked like?

'What sort of tour is it?' Morgan asked, still looking at the note.

'I'm the support act for an American country singer. Twelve concerts in just under three weeks.'

Morgan looked up. 'What's the name of the singer?'

'Someone not very well known. Calista Shaw.'

'Calista Shaw?' Morgan dropped the note on the desk. 'I've got both of her albums!'

'You're joking! I'd never really heard of her until the other day.'

'I'm a big country music fan. She's done two albums. She's got long blonde hair. A bit of a looker.'

'You know a whole lot more than I do.'

'I'll have to drop you in a CD.'

'That would be great!'

They both started laughing. Jason couldn't believe the whole scene. Wait until he told Dave and Geoff about it. They wouldn't believe it either.

'Just wait here a moment,' Morgan said. 'I'll go and have a word with my boss.'

Jason waited for about ten minutes. He found himself walking around the office reading the posters and bulletins stuck on the wall. A few years ago he might have found it all quite interesting, but since the Gator affair his interest in crime had dipped. It was the same with TV shows. He had always watched crime shows like *NYPD Blue* and *Homicide*, but once he'd been on the receiving end of the real thing he couldn't watch them any more. He supposed it was a normal reaction that many people had been through, turning to nicer things once crime's ugly head had intruded into their peaceful lives.

When Morgan returned he said, 'You're a lucky man.' They both sat down again. 'Because of what happened last time with Phil Gator, Superintendent Cole doesn't want to take any chances. We'll put a watch on your house until Saturday and see if anything further happens. Then take it from there.'

Jason felt relieved. 'OK. That would be a weight off my mind. Who will you send?'

'I'll send Beech down and someone else. They can do twelve-hour shifts. If it's all right with you, I'd like to install them in your house. They'll be in plain clothes. Maybe they could sit in the living room, out of the way?'

Jason thought of Dave and his obsessive TV-watching. It would be quite amusing to have a policeman in there with him. 'That'll be fine,' he said. 'When will they come round?'

'Right away. An hour or so.'

'Great. Thanks for your help.'

'No problem,' Morgan said. 'I'll put a CD through the letterbox. Naughton Road, isn't it? Which number?'

'Number eight.'

Morgan smiled. 'It would be great if you could get Calista to sign it for me.'

Jason had to chuckle to himself as he walked back down the hill towards his house. A country-music-loving policeman! He'd never heard of such a thing, but supposed most policemen were normal human beings. Maybe this would be the start of a beautiful friendship.

He was also looking forward to seeing PC Beech again. She had come to his house on Monday evening as soon as he'd rung about the brick incident. She was slightly taller than him, and had managed the near-impossible act of looking sexy in her uniform. She had short dark hair and a pretty face, and reminded him of Teri Hatcher, the American actress who played Lois Lane, Superman's love interest on TV. But she was a lot younger than Jason's forty-one. Probably in her mid-twenties. He started fantasizing about having a relationship with her. Her handcuffs could come in useful.

His house was only half a mile from the police station, so Jason was back indoors in no time. He went downstairs to the basement where he kept all his guitars and teaching equipment. He wanted to rehearse some songs for the tour and clear his mind of that second note.

The note had read, 'The ghost of Gator returns', and it had certainly got Morgan's attention. Jason supposed it was some friend of Gator's coming to get revenge for his friend's death. He wished Frankie Bosser was around again to protect him, but he hadn't heard from Frankie in over a year. They had written to each other a few times since '95, but like most things it had fizzled out after a while. Jason's letters had always been much longer than Frankie's, as well. He could tell Frankie wasn't much of a letter writer, he was too much of a tough guy for that sort of thing.

Jason plugged in his Martin guitar and strummed through a few songs. His heart wasn't really in it, though, and after five minutes he decided to stop. He left the cellar and went upstairs to the living room. He would sit and wait for PC Beech to arrive instead.

5

He saw her driving up about thirty minutes later. She parked a light grey Ford Escort on the street outside, opened the front gate and walked up the garden path. Her uniform was gone and she was in faded blue jeans and a light brown jumper. Jason couldn't take his eyes off her legs as she walked towards him. She looked like some kind of vision.

He walked into the hallway and opened the front door. 'We meet again,' he said, giving her his friendliest smile, trying to show that he wasn't the stressed-out idiot she'd met the other night.

She smiled back but without the same kind of enthusiasm. She was carrying a briefcase, which she held up in front of him. 'I've brought some paperwork along and a book to read. Show me where I can put myself.'

He led her into the living room and felt a bit ashamed about the old sofa and armchairs, the worn carpet on the floor. He had hoovered after the brick incident, though, and the smashed window was now boarded up.

'No new glass yet?' Beech asked.

'They'll be coming tomorrow, but that's what they said yesterday,' Jason said. 'Will this be all right for you? You've got the TV and stereo. I thought if you sat in this armchair you'd be hidden from sight.' He pointed to one of the armchairs that he'd pushed back into a corner. It was well hidden from anyone on the street.

PC Beech nodded. 'That'll be fine.' She set her briefcase down on it.

Jason led her into the kitchen to show her the tea-making

facilities, and then showed her the rest of the house so she knew the exact layout. She told him to call her Julie unless there was another policeman around, in which case he should revert to PC Beech. Jason nearly said, Can't I just call you gorgeous? but managed to keep his mouth shut.

Down in the basement Julie looked at his guitars with some interest, along with his Korg electric piano and microphones.

'I've always wanted to play the piano,' she said, 'but never had the time to learn.'

'That's what everyone says,' Jason told her, 'but the truth is, if you wanted to learn you'd have made the time.'

She looked at him as if she'd just been told off, and it was his first glimpse of the policewoman front dropping away.

'Can you play something for me?' she asked, gesturing towards the piano.

'Of course,' Jason said. 'What sort of music do you like?' He stepped over to the piano stool and sat down.

'Van Morrison and Bob Dylan.'

Jason nearly fell off the stool. 'You're joking?'

'Why shouldn't I like them? Just because I'm young doesn't mean I have to like Oasis. I can't stand them, in fact.'

'You're a woman after my own heart,' Jason said.

Julie said, 'Most of today's music is derivative. It's all been done before. Oasis just sound like a bad imitation of The Beatles to me. I'd rather have the real thing.'

Jason looked down at the keyboard. 'Me too. Well, I don't know any Van the Man, but I know plenty of Dylan. Any particular favourites?'

'Play what you like. I know most of them.'

Jason pulled a microphone down in front of him, threw a few switches and told Julie to sit down. She sat about ten feet away among his guitars and music stands. Playing to one person was just about the perfect audience as far as Jason was concerned, and when he was on stage he tried to imagine a similar situation. He felt back in control of things now, a feeling that had been the other way round on Monday night when Julie had been investigating the broken window.

He played the opening chords of 'Ballad Of A Thin Man', and Julie nodded in recognition. It was a great song to sing, and Jason really hammered it up on the chorus. When it was over, Julie applauded and asked for another, so he did a slow version of 'I Want You'. Suddenly the pleading chorus took on a whole new meaning, and he had to look away from Julie as he repeated, 'I want you' over and over. He felt a little embarrassed when he'd finished.

'That was great!' Julie said. 'You should be on the stage.'

'Well, now that you mention it . . .' Jason said, and then he told her all about the forthcoming Calista Shaw tour.

In the Red Lion pub, just over the road from Woodvale police station, Jesse Morgan was drinking a soda with ice, watching with jealousy as Ian Kiddie sipped a half of lager. It was early evening, and they were taking a brief break before getting back to the murder at the Bell's Plastics factory.

'That tastes good, does it?' Kiddie teased.

'Refreshing,' Morgan said. 'I'll be clear-headed when we go back to work, and you won't.'

'What's this, Day Number Two?'

'That's right. One day at a time is the way to do it.'

'You're hardly an alcoholic.'

'You should see what I put away at home.'

Morgan's old girlfriend Nicola appeared behind the bar and smiled at him. Their affair had lasted about seven months, starting in the summer of 1995. They began dating when the Gator murders had just been getting under way, and started sleeping together when the case was over. At the time Morgan had thought she was the woman for him, but as the months passed by he found himself losing interest, until finally the whole thing was just depressing him. He broke the relationship up and managed to blame it on his job, like he always did. Well, he wouldn't have that excuse any more, and things would have to change.

He hadn't been out with anyone since – nearly two years – and although he had slept with Nicola more than a few times since the split, he hadn't slept with her for about three months now. He felt more than a little horny looking at her in her black slacks and T-shirt, her shoulder-length dark hair. But he couldn't just ask her to go to bed with him. The situation would have to arise naturally, and they had hardly socialized recently, just the occasional phone call to see how the other was doing.

'A fine-looking woman,' Kiddie said, breaking into his thoughts. 'I don't know why you two don't try again.'

Morgan looked at his friend. Kiddie had been happily married for years, and instead of children had a Labrador called Spotless. He was one of the most contented people Morgan had ever met, and he often envied him. But he didn't want to get on to the Nicola subject at that moment.

'So what did you find out about Jim Brady?' he asked abruptly, and Kiddie got the hint.

'Well, he was inside all right, but only for skipping alimony payments. He was on his third wife when he was killed. His new wife is only in her thirties. And a bit of a looker, according to Brazier, who went over to give her the bad news.'

'How did she take it?'

'He thought she was a bit calm about it, but then he thought she was a bit of a tough nut as well.'

'Sounds like maybe we should concentrate on her then.'

'That's what Brazier thought.'

Morgan sipped his soda. It tasted horrible. 'How long was Brady inside?'

'Six months. But this was quite a while ago. He's been at Bell's for eight years or so. Went to work there when he came out. Before that he was a publican. Ran a pub called The Duke of Wellington in north London. That was with his second wife. He got put in jail for not paying alimony to the first wife and the two kids he had with her. When he went inside he lost his job and the second wife.'

'This is complicated. I wonder if he kept in contact with any criminals.'

'Not that we know of. It's amazing how complicated some people make their lives.'

'You're telling me.'

'So he comes out of jail, starts working at Bell's and marries wife number three. Met her at the local Conservative Club. She has two kids from her first marriage and they live with her.'

Morgan shook his head. 'Jesus. I'm glad I never had any kids.'

'Me too. I'm happy with Spotless.'

Morgan chuckled. He called Nicola over and she poured out another half of lager for Kiddie.

'Same again for you?' she asked.

'No, I'll have a ginger ale this time.'

'You ought to be careful, mixing your drinks.'

He paid her and their eyes met briefly. Morgan wondered if it was a loaded look, or if he was just imagining things.

'So,' Morgan said, when Nicola had walked away, 'we start looking back at the wife's past as well. This could take more than a few days.'

'It'll keep you off the streets,' Kiddie said.

'And keep my mind off the drink.' He screwed up his face as he sipped his ginger ale.

6

On Thursday morning Teddy Peppers awoke to the sound of someone knocking on his door. He looked at the watch on his bedside table and saw that it was ten o'clock.

'Who is it?' he shouted.

'It's the maid, come to do your room.'

'No need, I'll do it myself!'

He heard a muffled 'OK' and lay back down on the pillows. Fucking hell! What did a man have to do to get some peace?

Since getting out of prison a week ago, Teddy had been struggling to have a lie-in in every bed and breakfast or hotel he had been staying in. This was the fourth, and it had been the same everywhere: a knock on the door every morning, trying to get him out of bed. He couldn't understand the attraction of these places if they kicked you out so early. It was like being back in jail again. Wasn't the whole point of staying in a hotel so that you didn't have to get up at the crack of dawn? In these places you had to get up with the birds just to catch breakfast. He would have to find somewhere else to live where there were no maids and he had his own kitchen.

He couldn't get back to sleep now that his brain was ticking over, so he climbed out of bed and walked naked to the small shower cubicle. He pulled back the curtain and saw that, like the last two B&Bs he'd stayed in, it was one of those electric showers with a complicated system of knobs and one lever. He swore out loud and stood there fiddling with them until eventually he got a piddly little trickle coming out at roughly the right heat. He stepped under, wishing for the explosive blast he'd been used to for the past seven years in Headstone Prison.

He washed his dyed, pale orange cropped hair with the shampoo provided, which was in a tube about the size of his little finger. When that was done he washed himself with the bar of soap which was about the size of two squares of a Yorkie bar. Teddy was getting used to everything in miniature. It was like being a bit player in a doll's house drama. Even the towels were small, more like the size of your average tea towel.

After he'd dried himself he slapped on some deodorant and dressed in black jeans and a cream denim shirt. He pulled on his new black cowboy boots and then his hip-length black leather jacket, both bought just yesterday on a stolen credit card.

Standing in front of the mirror, he thought he looked quite youthful for a thirty-five-year-old. He had never liked his nose, which was just a little too large for his face, but he was still a good-looking boy. His skin was a bit too pale after years inside, though, but that couldn't be helped.

He left his room and walked down the carpeted corridor to the stairs. He walked out of the front door without seeing anyone, and on to the pavement, which was at the far end of Woodvale High Street. To his left the road stretched away towards countryside and a golf course, so the lady at reception had informed him. As if he looked like a golfer.

He turned right instead and headed towards Woodvale, the town he had arrived in just four days ago. A rumbling in his stomach told him he needed to get some breakfast, so he started looking for a café.

It felt good to be walking around in everyday clothes again, among the so-called normal people, and also more than a little strange; Teddy had been in jail almost all his adult life from the age of twenty-two.

His first spell had been for five years for taking part in a series of robberies at pubs in south-east London. It was a good scam while it lasted, and had netted his gang of four over fifty thousand pounds for the three successful robberies they'd pulled off.

The gang would turn up at a pub on a Monday morning, one of them dressed as a uniformed sergeant, the other three posing as plain-clothes policemen. Showing a phoney warrant to the publican, they would say they had arrived to search the premises for drugs. The publican would be distracted while the gang searched the place, and when he handed over the safe keys, they would clean out the week-end's takings. They would take the keys with them to delay the publican discovering his loss, and disappear into the London suburbs.

The plan had worked three times, but on the fourth occasion they had been caught out by a publican's wife who had used a mobile phone in her bedroom to alert the police when she thought something strange was going on downstairs. Publicans all over London had been warned about the gang, and had been waiting for them to try it again.

When he came out of jail after that first stretch, Teddy soon became bored with trying to go straight, and fell in with another group of criminals: armed robbers. Their speciality was armoured vans, and then later, food superstores. The one Teddy got caught for was a Safeway's, where he was left behind at the scene.

There were four of them involved in that one too, and using a stolen Range Rover, they had rammed through the glass doors before the store had opened early one morning. Wearing black masks and waving shotguns at stunned staff, they had emptied all the safes within minutes, but as they made their escape, Teddy had run right into a gung-ho sales assistant. The assistant had tackled him by the legs and then hung on for dear life, even as Teddy bashed him around the face with the butt of his shotgun. Eventually managing to free himself, Teddy had run outside only to see the getaway car disappearing in the distance. The police had caught him running down the road looking very much like the village idiot. One of his aims in a few weeks' time was to find the other gang members and try to get back some of the money he was owed for not grassing them up. It was a bit of a long shot after seven years, and although he felt it was something he deserved, it would have to wait until more pressing matters were out of the way first.

Teddy found a café and sat by the window waiting to be served. Yes, he thought. He certainly had a busy few weeks in front of him.

At about the same time on Thursday morning, Jesse Morgan and Ian Kiddie were driving over to Horley to have their first interview with Jim Brady's wife, Monica. They had tried to see her last night but she had been visiting relatives, no doubt consoling her over her recent loss.

Horley was just a ten-minute drive from Woodvale, a town which didn't have much to offer except its close proximity to Gatwick Airport.

The Brady home was a bungalow on the outskirts, up a side road, one of nine bungalows all in a row. The other side of the street was just a field, and the gardens of the bungalows were unfenced and looked unfinished and bare, as if the residents couldn't be bothered cultivating them. They parked outside the Brady house and Kiddie said, 'What a strange street.'

'Exactly what I was thinking,' Morgan said. 'Like someone left when the job was only half done.'

They climbed from the car and walked up a cement path that ran through the bare front lawn. There were no flower beds or shrubs or trees, just a child's bicycle lying on its side.

Morgan rang the bell twice and eventually a tall woman with short, dyed-blonde hair opened the door. She had a cigarette in her left hand and Morgan could smell whisky on her breath. He flashed his ID and she reluctantly let them in.

They followed her down a wooden-floored passage into the living room.

It was a sparse room, with crimson linoleum on the floor and a dark green leather three-piece suite. On a glass coffee table sat a half-empty bottle of whisky, some magazines and an overflowing ashtray. In the corner was one of those gigantic TVs which Morgan hated, with a video underneath. The TV dominated the room and Ian Kiddie made small talk about it as Morgan glanced quickly around. There were a few pictures on the walls, a sideboard with family photos and a small dining table with four cheap chairs around it. The room had a cold, empty feel, and Morgan was glad he didn't have to live in such a place.

Morgan and Kiddie sat on the sofa while Monica Brady sat in the armchair. She had a short dress on, and wasn't shy about flashing her long, tanned muscular legs. She leaned back in her seat and said, 'So what would you like to know?' It was more of a challenge than a question.

Morgan sat in silence while Kiddie ran through the usual mundane questions. He found it hard not to look at Monica Brady's legs, which were always a big attraction for him in a woman. She had slender arms and long, thin fingers, the ones on her left hand nicotine-stained. Her hair came down to her shoulders and curled inwards at the bottom; her long thin face was quite wrinkled for someone in her mid-thirties. Her teeth were nicotine-stained as well, and her mouth curled down at the edges, suggesting the mouth of a bitter person who didn't smile much. Morgan was wondering where the two children were until she told them they were at her parents'. She said she needed time to be on her own, time to get drunk and wallow in self-pity.

'Have you any idea who might have done this?' Kiddie eventually asked.

Monica Brady shook her head. 'If I knew who'd done it I would've told that last copper who came round. Either that, or I'd be out there catching him myself.'

Morgan wasn't surprised to hear the impatience creeping into her voice. He was surprised she had held out this long. 'Can I ask you about your ex-husband?' he said. 'Do you think he could've had anything to do with it?'

'I very much doubt it,' she said. 'My ex has been in jail for the past seven years.'

Morgan perked up. 'In jail, for what?'

'Armed robbery.'

'And this was when? Back in 1990?'

'Yeah. That was a year to remember. But looking back, it was a bit of a godsend, really. It was a good way of getting rid of him.'

'You didn't get on then?'

'That's a bit of an understatement. We hated each other's guts.'

Morgan smiled. 'Well, we'd better check him out just the same. What's his name?'

'Teddy,' Monica Brady said. 'But he sure isn't cute and cuddly.'

'Teddy what?'

'Teddy Peppers. Hot and spicy and sure to get up your nose if you breathe in too close to him.'

'And what jail is he meant to be in?'

'Headstone, the last I heard. But who knows? They might have moved him somewhere else.'

Kiddie was taking everything down, and after a few more questions Morgan decided they had enough to be getting on with. They left her sitting with a cigarette and let themselves out.

When they were back in the car Kiddie said, 'What do you reckon?'

'I reckon we check out Teddy Peppers,' Morgan said. 'Apart from that, I don't know.'

'A nice pair of legs, though,' Kiddie said.

'I didn't think you noticed such things.'

'I may be happily married, but I'm still a man.'

'Well, nobody's perfect.'

Morgan turned on the ignition and drove away from the bungalows.

7

On the other side of the street from 8 Naughton Road, there was a public footpath that threaded its way through hedges and trees. You could walk along the footpath and not be seen from the other side of the road, so it was the perfect place to watch number eight from. This had been Teddy Peppers's hiding place on Monday night, when he had sat for a couple of hours waiting for Jason Campbell to come home. Because it had been dark, he had been able to climb into a tree and sit on a branch unnoticed. The branch had become a bit uncomfortable, but he had been able to change position regularly, and in a bumbag had a packet of Hobnobs and a small bottle of mineral water to keep him sustained.

Teddy knew roughly what Jason Campbell looked like from his conversations in jail with Karl Spoiler. Spoiler had been Phil Gator's last partner in crime, his accomplice in a post office robbery they had both botched up. Spoiler had managed to escape from Woodvale at the time, but had been picked up in Brighton a few weeks later, where he was fast running out of the thousand pounds he had managed to get away with. He had eventually ended up in the same prison as Teddy, and Teddy had learned the whole sorry story of how Gator had met his fate in the house on Naughton Road.

Back in 1992, when Gator had briefly been in Headstone jail, Teddy had been his cell-mate and fuck-friend. Teddy had been a normal heterosexual before he started his seven-year sentence, but by the time Gator arrived in his cell he was regularly fucking other men. At first, Gator, who was such a typical macho hoodlum, had been very wary of him, avoiding his constant advances, but in such a tiny cell there was nowhere to hide. Eventually Teddy seduced him one quiet evening, when at last he managed to break Gator's resistance.

For the last five months of Gator's incarceration they had fucked each other ragged, and when Gator had finally been set free Teddy had been surprised at how much he missed him. He had fucked other men afterwards, but nothing had been as exciting as deflowering the virgin Gator. When he learned of Gator's death from the TV news and newspapers, he had been devastated. When Karl had told him all the extra details that the papers had left out, he had sworn to get revenge for his old friend when he finally got out of jail. And Jason Campbell was the top name on his list.

Teddy knew that Jason Campbell hadn't really been the man who had killed Gator, but for now he would have to do. The person really responsible was some old criminal whose name Teddy didn't know. The criminal had vanished to Europe and the papers hadn't named him, but Gator had been killed inside Campbell's house, and Campbell had been there when it happened: so that was a good enough reason for him to die.

Teddy watched the house now from the secluded footpath and wondered if he could get into the back garden instead. Being daylight, there were too many people wandering up and down the path, and climbing into a tree was certainly out of the question. He had a Beretta pistol in his inside jacket pocket and a flick knife strapped to his ankle, both bought on his second day of freedom from an acquaintance in London. He walked along the path until there was a gap, stepped out on to Naughton Road, and then walked slowly back towards number eight.

Jason was fixing a few sandwiches in the kitchen as PC Julie Beech watched him. He was a bit of a pâté freak, and would often walk into Woodvale just for the sole purpose of buying some from Batchelor's delicatessen. Today he had some good chunky liver with pineapple in it, and he was fixing Julie a side salad as well. She was on her second day shift in his house, and would be there until six in the evening when Sergeant Brazier would take over, an overweight, genial policeman, who held far less fascination for Jason.

After singing those two songs to Julie yesterday, she had left him in the basement to rehearse, and gone to the living room to keep an eye out for strangers. Jason had wanted to chat to her some more, but didn't want to interfere with her work. When he'd taken her a cup of tea and biscuits at four o'clock, however, she had seemed keen for some company, and they'd sat and talked until Brazier had arrived. Jason had left Brazier to sit in front of the TV on his own, and when Dave had returned from the swimming pool he had kept him company, two TV freaks together.

In the last few days Jason had made phone calls to his guitar students to cancel any forthcoming lessons. They had all been pleased to hear his big news and wished him well.

'Are you looking forward to the tour?' Julie asked him now.

'It'll make a nice change,' Jason said. 'It can get a bit claustrophobic working from home all the time. Most people think it's the ideal job, but it can drive you up the wall as well.' He sliced some tomatoes and put them on a bed of lettuce.

'I couldn't do it,' Julie said.

'I suppose your job is the complete opposite. Always on the move. Always talking to people.'

'It has its boring side too. You try walking the beat in Woodvale for eight hours. All you get is people asking directions,' she laughed.

Jason thought Julie had the most appealing laugh he'd heard for a long time. She had told him yesterday that she was twenty-five and had joined the force at the age of nineteen. She had been posted to Charing Cross police station in London for five years, and had been transferred to Woodvale only last year. She liked leafy Surrey, supposedly one of the wealthiest counties in England.

Jason was pouring some dressing over the salad when Julie said, 'What was that?'

He stopped what he was doing and turned to look at her tense face. The atmosphere had suddenly changed and Julie was listening for something. 'There's a noise coming from the basement,' she said, and then she was gone.

Jason stood rooted to the spot, not knowing what to do. He looked out of the window that was directly above the basement door that led into the back garden. He couldn't see anything. Or could he?

He quickly grabbed a stool, stood on that, and with the extra height could see a man at the basement door. The man had short ginger hair and he seemed to be trying to get in!

Jason nearly fell off the stool trying to get out of sight. He rushed out of the kitchen, into the hallway, and started down the basement stairs. He could hear voices as he went down, then a scream and a scuffle.

He stopped in his tracks, remembering his previous basement incident with Gator, and the broken thumb he'd received because of it. But then he thought of Julie and continued down the stairs.

Teddy Peppers was getting out of there quick.

He had been fiddling with the basement door when it had suddenly sprung open and a dark-haired young woman was standing in front of him. He had been about to go into some bullshit story when she pulled out a police badge and shoved it in his face. Teddy had done the only thing he could in such a situation, which was punch her on the nose. She had hit the floor, no problem, blood spurting out everywhere.

Now he was walking down the front drive, not too quick but quick enough, not looking back over his shoulder, which was the worst thing you could do, let someone get a peek at your face.

But the policewoman had got a peek at his face! Shit, he thought, and carried on walking.

When he got to the basement, Jason saw Julie lying on the cement floor, blood all over her face. He rushed over and knelt by her side. She was conscious but moaning softly. Her nose was all squashed and he felt incredibly sorry for her. He could tell it was broken and knew there was nothing you could do to fix it. She would be disfigured for life.

He ran back upstairs, picked up the phone in the hallway and dialled 999. Then he went to the kitchen and put some warm water in a bowl and grabbed a clean J-Cloth. His hands were shaking and he felt like a nervous wreck. He managed to get back to the basement without spilling too much water, and knelt beside Julie as he wiped the blood off her. A few minutes later he heard a police siren and knew that the cavalry was coming.

8

It was Friday morning around eleven o'clock, when Jesse Morgan found himself walking down the corridor to Chief Superintendent Cole's office. He sat down opposite the younger man and waited for him to look up from his paperwork. Cole looked freshly shaven as usual but was losing his hair rapidly, something that always pleased Morgan.

Cole looked up with a serious expression and asked, 'How is Julie Beech?'

'She's still in hospital,' Morgan said. 'Looks a mess. She's got a broken nose, I'm afraid.'

'A terrible shame. Such a nice-looking girl. Was it you who put her on that detail? If so, why her? Shouldn't we have used a male officer?'

'In hindsight I suppose we should. I chose her because she was the one who answered Campbell's call on Monday evening. I put her on the day shift because I expected nothing to happen. Brazier was on the night shift.'

Morgan felt very guilty about Julie. He had been to see her in hospital last night and had been shocked by her appearance. Apart from the broken nose, she had two black eyes and lots of swelling. She looked as if she'd gone a few rounds with Lennox Lewis. It must've been one hell of a punch she'd been struck with. She had given a description of her attacker, but it wasn't much to go on. She had only seen him for a few seconds. Now all the local bobbies were looking for ginger-haired men who looked like tough guys, and pulling them in for questioning.

'Yes, hindsight is something we could all do with,' Cole said, and Morgan wondered if that was meant to be some kind of profound statement. 'I've been thinking about this since it happened, and I've come up with an alternative.'

Morgan held his breath. He had a feeling something bad was going to come out of his boss's mouth. Like maybe the short end of a stick.

'We'll keep Brazier and one other, a man this time, at the Naughton Road house, but I want you to travel with Jason Campbell when he goes on this infernal tour tomorrow.'

'Come again?' Morgan said. He couldn't believe what he was hearing.

'I want you to travel with Campbell. He's obviously going to be in some kind of danger as he travels, and I don't want to carry the can if he gets attacked somewhere up north. I know you're a fan of country music, so it should be the ideal job for you.'

'What about the Brady murder?'

'We'll leave Hickle and Kiddie in charge of that one. It looks as though it may take some time, anyway. No strong leads so far, are there?'

'No, but . . .'

'It'll be a nice change of scenery for you. If you really are going to leave in two months, I may as well let someone else run the murder enquiry. This'll be a nice little break for you.'

Morgan smiled ruefully. 'Well, it'll certainly be different.'

They talked some more about the finer details, then Morgan was out of there and back in his office, clearing paperwork from his desk. He walked downstairs and out through reception. He would have to telephone Kiddie later, and he supposed he would have to ring Nicola as well. She would only get annoyed if he left without telling her.

He jumped in his car and drove down the hill to 8 Naughton Road. Another policeman, Hoad, who had taken over the day shift from Beech, met him at the door.

'How's Julie?' Hoad asked as he let him in.

'Not too great, I'm afraid,' Morgan said. 'And the good news is you've landed her detail for good.'

'Great,' Hoad said without enthusiasm. 'What am I going to do here for twelve hours every day?'

'You've got a TV in there, bring in some videos. Sounds like a cushy number to me.' Morgan watched the light go on in Hoad's head. He was a fanatical West Bromwich Albion supporter, a Birmingham man who had married a Londoner and ended up in Surrey. Morgan knew he had a large collection of West Brom videos. He also knew that in winter Hoad wore a West Brom football shirt underneath his uniform.

'That's a good idea,' Hoad said, with a satisfied smile.

'Where's Jason Campbell?' Morgan asked.

'Down in the basement. He sounds good. Not that I know anything about that kind of music.'

'I've never heard him, but it seems I'll be hearing a lot more of him soon. I've been assigned to be his personal bodyguard on his tour.'

'You're joking! I can't imagine you as a roadie.'

'Well, I don't plan on carrying his guitars for him.'

'It could be interesting.'

'Should be. I'll go down and give him the news.'

Morgan listened to the music as he made his way down the stairs. Campbell had a nice, pleasing voice, fairly deep, and he was playing a slow ballad. He stopped in mid-song as soon as he saw Morgan, a slightly embarrassed look coming to his face.

'Sounds good,' Morgan said. 'How are you feeling after yesterday?'

'I could be feeling better,' Jason said. 'I just feel so bad about Julie. I went to see her this morning. She looks a real mess.'

'An unfortunate incident,' Morgan said. 'But these things happen.'

He went and sat on a chair opposite Jason. He had been down here once before, after the Gator affair two years ago. 'It seems you've acquired more instruments since I was last here,' he said looking around. 'More guitars. And a mandolin.' There were about ten guitars hanging from the walls on special brackets. Morgan thought they made nice ornaments.

'It's a bit addictive,' Jason said. 'I see a flash-looking one and I have to have it. They're not very expensive. Half of them don't even play very well.'

'How many will you take on tour?'

'As I'm going by train, I'll take just the one. This one.' He patted the guitar on his lap. 'If I were driving I would take two. I'd feel more comfortable with two, in case something happens to one of them.'

'Why aren't you driving?'

'The first gig is in Glasgow, tomorrow night. I don't want to be driving for eight hours and then have to perform. I'd rather just sit on a train. So for the northern part of the tour I'll be taking trains. I'll start driving when it comes back down south.'

'Well, you *could* take two guitars up north.'

'How do you mean?'

'I've just been told I'll be coming with you for added protection. I'll carry one, if you like.' Morgan remembered Hoad's remark about being a roadie.

Jason smiled, and Morgan thought there was more than a little relief in it. 'That would be great! I've been feeling on edge all week. I have visions of this guy shooting me on stage.'

'I wouldn't start thinking those kinds of thoughts or you'll never get up there. But we have to take his threat seriously, especially after what's happened to Julie, and bearing in mind he was a friend of Phil Gator.'

'I'm certainly taking it seriously. It'll be great to have you along.'

Morgan reached in his pocket. 'This is the CD I was going to get Calista Shaw to sign. I'll be able to do that myself now, but this is what she looks like.' He handed the CD over.

'A nice-looking woman,' Jason said.

'She certainly is. I can't wait to meet her.'

'Can I borrow this for tonight? I'll give it back tomorrow.'

'Sure. What train are you catching?'

'I'm getting the nine o'clock from King's Cross. Gets into Glasgow just before three. It's a slow one, but it was cheaper than the fast one. It'll cost you quite a bit if you haven't already booked a ticket.'

'I won't have to pay a thing. I'm a policeman, remember.'

They sat and talked a bit more about where to meet the next day and then Morgan went back upstairs. He chatted to Hoad for a while and told him that Brazier would be back as usual at six.

'I don't know if anything else will happen here if Jason's on the road,' Hoad said.

'Yes, but the stalker doesn't know that, does he? Or not yet, anyway. I'm sure he'll find out somehow. I want to know about anyone who comes round asking questions.'

'OK. I'll keep my eyes peeled.'

Walking back to his car, Jesse Morgan almost felt light-headed. No boring weekend work for him. Tomorrow he would be meeting Calista Shaw!

9

On Thursday afternoon, after he'd punched the police-woman's lights out, Teddy Peppers had walked quickly back to his bed and breakfast, picking up some dark brown hair dye along the way. Back in his room he had stood over the bathroom sink and rubbed the stuff into his hair. It was a messy process and took a long time getting it looking exactly right, but it was something that had to be done. Every policeman in Woodvale would be on the lookout for an orange-haired tough nut.

As he rubbed the dye in, he wondered if his parents would be looking out for him as well. They lived down in Hastings, and he had sent them a postcard from London telling them he was now a free man. But he had more urgent things to do before going back to his home town, and family reunions could wait. He had already concluded part one of his mission in this part of the country, and he was sure he could wrap up part two in the next few days. OK, so Jason Campbell now had cops at his house, but that was just another little problem he would have to work around.

If he'd been smart, he wouldn't have put the warning notes through Campbell's window and letterbox; they had announced his presence in the area, warned that he had something to do with Gator, and had subsequently led to the police being in Campbell's house. Instead, he could've just gone in unannounced, done the deed and then disappeared. But it was too late now. And anyway, it would be more of a challenge now that the filth was involved.

After dyeing his hair, he decided to go out for some

evening's entertainment, see what it was like being a dark-haired man in this world. Teddy's natural colour was blond, but he had dyed it orange as soon as he'd got out of jail, not because he liked the colour, but as a statement of freedom. Now because of unforeseen circumstances, he could be dark for a while. He wondered if his character would change with it as he changed into a completely black outfit as well: jeans, T-shirt, V-necked sweater and cowboy boots. With his black leather jacket draped over his shoulder, he thought he looked pretty mean, but hopefully not too mean to pick up a spare woman.

He left his room at eight o'clock, and downstairs asked the middle-aged receptionist if there were any good pubs within walking distance. She pointed towards the golf course, looking at him strangely, trying to figure out what was different. Teddy supposed he'd better move on quite soon.

Heading left out of the B&B, Teddy was looking forward to a couple of pints after the day's excitement. He walked with a spring in his step, not easy in cowboy boots, and soon saw some golfing greens with flagpoles sticking out of them. He turned up a narrow country road with woods on either side, and asked directions from an old couple walking their dog. They pointed him up a rutted road, the golf course stretching away on either side.

After about five more minutes of walking in the dark, Teddy saw the pub at the top of a small rise, cars parked on either side of the road. He was wishing he wasn't wearing his cowboy boots now, because the road was so rough he was almost turning his ankle with each step. But he made it to the front door without injury and stepped inside.

The pub was already quite crowded, full of the trendy middle-classes sipping their pints and eating pasties with brown sauce on the side. The pasties looked pretty good to Teddy, so to blend right in he ordered one for himself, along with a pint of bitter and a whisky. He squeezed on to a stool at the bar and watched the barmaids while he waited for his pasty, which rotated in front of him in a microwave. When it was ready he poured some brown sauce and English mustard on to his plate and ate with his fingers. He washed it down with a few sips of beer, which tasted a bit like warm mud, but when you've been in prison for seven years almost anything tastes good.

When the pasty was nestling pleasantly in his belly, Teddy turned around and surveyed the evening's crowd. The pub looked like someone's living room: there were armchairs all over the place, in different shapes and colours, and the walls were full of prints of horses and golfers and country houses. In the far corner a group of people were playing a pub game Teddy had never seen before. It consisted of trying to throw a small hoop that hung from the ceiling on a piece of cord, on to an animal's horn that was fixed to the wall some ten feet away. Teddy watched transfixed as the players swung the hoop in an arc, hoping to land it on the horn. They were all hopeless, and after about ten minutes of watching, only one person had been successful. Surely it couldn't be that difficult.

Teddy threw his whisky back in one, picked up his beer and walked over. 'Mind if I have a go?' he asked them. There were two men and three women playing. Teddy had already figured out who the spare woman was, a shortish blonde a little on the plump side with a big chest, who looked to be about fifty or so. He smiled at her and she returned it with interest.

'Well, er, all right,' one of the men said reluctantly. He was short with a fair moustache. Teddy couldn't see the point of growing a fair moustache. The man was a loser. He handed the hoop to Teddy and started to explain the throwing action.

'I've been watching you for ten minutes,' Teddy interrupted, 'and I hardly think you're the one to give me lessons.'

The others laughed and the man backed away with a

hurt expression. He could feel his manhood being stepped upon.

Teddy took the hoop and felt its weight. It was about three inches in diameter. He had always been a pretty good knife thrower, ever since he was a boy, so he thought this should be no problem at all. He faced the horn on the wall with a slight sideways stance and then swung the hoop in a gentle arc. The hoop went up, and on its backward swing landed squarely on top of the horn.

Teddy punched the air. The others in the group cheered, and Fair Moustache looked flummoxed. The woman he was with, a dumpy redhead, looked embarrassed to be with such a twerp.

'Beginner's luck,' Fair Moustache said. 'I bet you can't do it again.'

Teddy smiled with venom at the little man and proceeded to land the hoop on the horn another nine times without missing once. As he did so, the crowd around them grew bigger, the cheers growing louder after each success, and Fair Moustache seemed to disintegrate before his eyes.

Teddy stopped. It seemed as if the whole pub was watching him now, and he didn't really want to draw so much attention to himself. He turned in the direction of the fifty-year-old blonde and said, 'Anyone want lessons?'

The blonde took the hint and came towards him, her breasts wobbling as she walked. Teddy put his arm around her when she reached him, and gave her waist a little squeeze. He whispered in her ear so the others couldn't hear: 'Now imagine that horn on the wall is me, and this,' he said, putting the hoop in her hand, 'is you.'

The rest had been easy: a quick ride back to the B&B in the blonde's Polo around ten o'clock, and then a quick ride on top of the blonde.

Her name was Vivian, and naked she was quite a tasty sight. It was a special treat to have a woman after seven years in jail. The looseness of her vagina made a nice change from all the tighter arseholes Teddy had been fucking, and it was also a lot cleaner. As he was about to come, Vivian told him that she'd had 'the operation', so it was safe to shoot off inside her. Teddy didn't know what 'the operation' was – half expecting one of her legs to fall off – but dutifully didn't withdraw.

Afterwards she told him a little about herself. She was fifty-two years old and didn't have to work any more because her ex-husband sent her a nice little cheque every month. He had left her when she was in her forties, and last year her only daughter had moved out too. She was basically a lonely person, looking for a man to liven up her life. Teddy heard alarm bells ringing when she'd said that, but when he got to thinking about it, thought that maybe she might come in useful. So he made love to her again, this time much slower, and ate some pussy for the first time since his late twenties.

Teddy had thought about giving Vivian a false name, like the name on the credit cards he had stolen, but decided that was too complicated. After all, he couldn't use those credit cards any more, and would soon have to find another batch. He couldn't change his name every time he got hold of some different ones.

Lying in bed, he thought about the muggings which had proved very profitable so far. The first had been on the train to London the day he'd left prison, and the second on the train down to Redgate on Monday. It had all been so easy, like taking candy from a baby.

His railway mugging routine was this: look for a first-class carriage with only one passenger inside, preferably a fat, suited businessman, punch passenger to an unconscious state, then take wallet and briefcase and alight at next station. Use credit cards as quickly as possible for immediate needs such as clothes, new sports bag and personal stereo, and then go to supermarkets to get cash-back on Switch cards. Teddy hadn't known about the cash-back routine until a couple of days before leaving prison, and it was certainly a profitable scam. It was amazing what you could pick up in jail. It was a mine of useful information.

So he decided to tell Vivian his real name, and that committed him to her. He didn't mind for the moment; he could do with some regular female company. He wasn't looking to fuck any more men now that he was out of prison.

Teddy spent the whole of Friday with Vivian as well, still mulling over punching the policewoman as they took a short drive to Box Hill for a picnic. Teddy had never been to Box Hill before, but Vivian said she had been to a boarding school near there. She drove them to the very top and they walked around, Teddy impressed with views of the River Mole and Mickleham Downs. There were lots of bikers around, and he felt a bit awkward walking with an older woman, especially when Vivian tried holding his hand. He got out of that one by saying he wasn't used to public shows of affection, which wasn't a lie considering he'd just come out of jail. He had told Vivian last night that he was a salesman by trade, in between jobs at the moment, and was in the Woodvale area looking up old friends.

In the late afternoon they drove back to Woodvale and over to Vivian's place so she could change her clothes. She obviously wasn't short of a bob or two, because her house was quite big and all her clothes looked brand new and fashionable. Teddy's eyes nearly popped out when she came downstairs wearing a black one-piece bodysuit, with a chunky zipper down the front, and black high-heeled boots. Teddy was on his feet immediately, pulling the zipper down to see what was underneath. When he saw the white lace underwear he almost went crazy with desire. He unpeeled the bodysuit and took her from behind over the dining-room table, Vivian's ample bottom and breasts giving him plenty to hold on to.

When they'd cleaned themselves up they went to the cinema in Woodvale to watch a film called *Grosse Pointe*

Blank. There was a young, good-looking guy playing the lead who was meant to be a hit man, but Teddy had met a few hit men in jail and they were all mean-looking bastards. He didn't believe the film for a second.

Afterwards, Vivian told him she'd enjoyed it, but Teddy told her he thought it was stupid. He wanted to tell her that he was a hit man himself, which in a way he was at the moment, and that he could take care of that punk on screen, no problem. He had already taken care of Jim Brady, and soon he would dispose of Jason Campbell.

When they were driving back to the B&B, he got Vivian to drive past the house on Naughton Road, and he saw that Campbell's blue Nissan was still parked outside. He wondered how many cops were still keeping watch. He decided that could be a job for Vivian.

So on Friday night he took her for a nice meal and then for a drink in a different country pub. When she was well juiced up he asked if she could do him a little favour the next morning. She reached over and squeezed his crotch in plain sight of several other drinkers, and said of course, she'd do anything for him.

Teddy wondered if that were true.

10

When the alarm went off at six o'clock on Saturday morning, Jason almost wished he could just reach over, turn it off and go back to sleep. He had hardly slept at all during the night, his mind working overtime worrying about the tour and the stalker on his tail. But he pushed himself out of bed and told himself to get on with it.

He felt a rush of adrenaline in his veins once he was awake, but being Cancerian, half of him just wanted to stay at home and teach guitar. He was also feeling apprehensive about that night's gig, which happened to be the biggest of the whole tour. He would be playing in front of fourteen hundred people at the Glasgow Royal Concert Hall, part of something called the Country Connections Festival, and the biggest audience he had played in front of to date was around two hundred. He couldn't imagine what it would feel like. He would just have to try to block out the vastness of the hall, and pretend he was singing in the Mojo Club. It would be a case of getting his mind right, and filling it with positive thoughts.

He had a quick wash and went downstairs to the hallway where his gear was packed and ready to go. He had two guitars and one sports bag crammed with clothes. He didn't bother with breakfast; there would be plenty of time to eat on the train.

The two policemen, Brazier and Hoad, were just changing shifts, and they helped him load up his car. Then Brazier scrounged a lift back to the police station where Jason had agreed to meet Jesse Morgan. The idea behind this was that if the Nissan was not parked at Naughton Road any more, then the stalker might not bother Dave and Geoff while Jason was away. So Jason was going to leave the Nissan at the police station.

Jesse Morgan was waiting for them when they got there, and after transferring everything to a police car, Brazier drove them to Redgate station. Morgan was dressed casually in jeans, sweater, trainers and brown suede jacket. He had one suitcase with him.

They got on the train at Redgate and chatted a little as it made its way to London. Morgan asked Jason what he thought of the Calista Shaw CD.

'Quite commercial,' Jason said. 'Almost like pop.'

'A lot of country is these days,' Morgan said. 'It sells by the bucketload.'

'I may have to lighten my set up a bit,' Jason said. 'Put in some of my less serious songs.'

'Do you do any cover versions?'

'A few. They usually go down better than my own songs.'

Morgan nodded. 'Everyone likes a good cover version.'

Jason still couldn't believe he was going on tour with a policeman. Morgan was obviously a big fan of this kind of music, so he would have to try to forget he was a copper and think of him as more of a security guard. He seemed an OK kind of guy, fairly serious and a thinker. He would like to hear some of his police stories, but they had plenty of time for that. Three weeks on the road together. They'd either be best friends by the end of it, or at each other's throats.

When Teddy Peppers woke up on Saturday morning, he had everything worked out. He would send Vivian over to Campbell's house posing as a prospective guitar student, and see if she could meet him and find out what his movements were. He told Vivian that Campbell was an old friend of his and he wanted to surprise him somewhere, walk into a restaurant, for instance, when Jason was eating, and say: Hi! Remember your old friend Teddy? Vivian believed this flimsy story, and because she wanted some excitement in her life was more than willing to go along with it.

But first of all they checked Teddy out of the B&B and drove all his stuff over to Vivian's house. There was no point in wasting money, and Teddy was rapidly running out of it.

It was about eleven o'clock when Vivian drove over to Naughton Road, Teddy staying behind in her house. He didn't want to risk being seen anywhere near the place, dyed hair or not.

She was back about thirty minutes later, and the first thing she said when she walked into the living room was, 'He's not there any more.'

Teddy said 'What!' a little too quickly and loudly, and Vivian gave him a funny look.

'He's not there any more,' she said. 'He's gone on a music tour. He'll be away for three weeks or so.'

'Shit!' Teddy said, trying to calm down. He couldn't hang around for three weeks.

'Well, you knew he was a guitar teacher,' Vivian said. 'But apparently he sings for a living as well. It seems this is his big breakthrough. His first tour. You should be pleased for him.'

'I am, I am,' Teddy said, remembering Jason was meant to be his buddy. 'I just would've liked to have seen the old bugger, that's all. Who did you speak to?'

'A tall chap with hardly any hair.'

That didn't sound like anyone Teddy had already seen going into the house back when he was watching it on Monday. Probably another cop.

'Did he say where he'd gone? Where the tour was going?'

'He said it was starting in Glasgow and the singer he was touring with was someone called Calista Shaw. Never heard of her myself.'

'Glasgow! Fucking hell! That's about as far away as it gets!'

'At least he hasn't gone to Europe or Japan.'

Teddy looked at Vivian to see if she was taking the piss. It seemed she wasn't. 'Yeah, always look on the bright side,' he said, slumping on to the sofa in a sulk.

'I've got an idea,' Vivian said, sitting down next to him and putting a hand on his knee. 'Why don't we go to a newsagent and buy every music magazine they have, and see if there's any mention of a Calista Shaw tour. If she's a big star, it'll be well advertised.'

'How do you know that?'

'Because they always are. Don't you ever notice them in newspapers and such? On the entertainments page? Lots of tours happen all the time. And they always tell you all the dates. I went to see Richard Clayderman last year. He did a very long tour.'

'Richard who?'

'He's a pianist. Obviously far too sophisticated for you.'

'Yeah, right. Well, if you think it's worth a shot, I'm game.'

'Of course it's worth a shot. Come on.'

She pulled him from the sofa and led him out of the living room. He felt like a little kid being dragged along by his mother. And, if he was truthful to himself, it wasn't such a bad feeling at all.

The train ride to Glasgow was long and monotonous. Because Jason had already reserved a seat and Jesse Morgan hadn't, Jason found himself sitting on his own surrounded by strangers. Morgan had told him that this wasn't such a bad idea, and that maybe they'd sit apart all the time just in case the stalker was watching them. This just put Jason back on edge, though, and he found himself looking at all the dodgy young men on board, wondering if one of them was his crazy attacker.

And there were plenty of dodgy people on board.

Because it was a Saturday morning, there were quite a few football fans travelling north to matches. Sitting just behind Jason was a group of middle-aged men talking about football in very loud voices. They certainly knew a lot about it, and were boring the whole carriage about the non-league variety, a subject Jason would've thought no one took any interest in. People started moving away from the men when spare seats became available, and there was an audible sigh of relief when they disembarked after about two hours.

Jason could see Jesse Morgan farther down the carriage. The big man was reading a newspaper first and then a paperback. He seemed to be enjoying the journey, chatting to some of the people around him, helping out a lady with her kids. Jason envied him. He seemed to be happy talking to people, being in their company. Jason was pretty much the opposite, a loner most of the time, although he did enjoy the company of his students.

The train pulled into Glasgow just before three. Jason climbed out with his guitar and made sure that Morgan was carrying his other one. He didn't trust anyone with his guitars, not even a policeman.

They had agreed that Jason should just act as if he were on his own and Morgan would follow along behind. So Jason headed for the exit and started looking for the Central Hotel where the concert's promoters had booked him in for the night, the only concert where that would be happening because it was part of a week-long festival. Not only was the room all paid for, the promoters had also agreed to pay for Jason's train fare. He was obviously in the big time now.

He found the Central Hotel in no time, right next to the station, hidden behind some scaffolding. At reception they ticked his name off a list and gave him a key. Jason saw Morgan sitting in the lobby, trying to look like a musician with Jason's guitar case next to him. Jason was startled to notice for the first time that Morgan looked a lot like Kris

Kristofferson. He wondered why he hadn't noticed that before.

As Jason passed him in the lobby, he flashed his key so Morgan would know which room he was in. Then he headed for the stairs.

The hotel was one of the biggest Jason had ever stayed in. The lengthy corridors reminded him of The Mirage Hotel in Las Vegas, which he'd stayed in once, although this hotel wasn't nearly so glamorous. The corridor just went on for ever, rooms on either side. He found his down a side corridor, and collapsed on to the bed. The phone beside him rang almost immediately.

'You safely installed?' It was Jesse Morgan.

'Safely installed,' Jason replied. 'I think I'll take a nap and a shower. Soundcheck is at five-thirty.'

'OK. I'll knock on your door at a quarter past. The concert hall's only up the road.'

'Sounds good to me. Don't forget the guitar.'

'What guitar?' Jesse Morgan said.

Then the line went dead.

11

In the guide to hotels and bed and breakfasts in Britain that Jesse Morgan had brought with him, it said that Glasgow was now a spruced-up, revamped, cultural and media capital, completely transformed from its original decaying, industrial, dead-end image. It said that this revival was ironic for such a traditionally socialist city, which now spent money on high-profile marketing campaigns and large-scale prestige projects and festivals, instead of more left-wing causes. Morgan found this description mildly annoying. Did the travel writer expect the city to stay the same for ever? Morgan was all for the cleaning-up and modernizing of cities; for a start it helped to keep crime down, and if it attracted tourists, extra income and jobs, then where was the harm in that? He put the book down in disgust on his bedside table and started getting ready to leave.

With guitar in hand he knocked on Jason's door at precisely five-fifteen. Jason let him in, looking freshly showered, wearing a black T-shirt with a collar, dark blue jeans and cowboy boots. He didn't have his glasses on, and Jason told him he never wore them on stage. It wasn't just vanity; the less he could see of the audience the better.

Morgan took a map out of his pocket and showed Jason the route to the concert hall. 'If you walk on ahead, I'll follow close behind.'

'You don't really think the stalker will be up here, do you?' Jason asked.

'I doubt it, but we can't be too careful. He probably hasn't found out about the tour yet, but I expect him to. Maybe he'll catch up with us in a few days.'

'Great. I can hardly wait to meet him.' Jason grabbed his coat and they walked out with the two guitars.

They split up as they reached the lobby, and Morgan glanced around to see if there was anyone watching them. Several people were, but he supposed they were looking to see if he was someone famous, a feeling Morgan found quite similar to when he arrived at a crime scene and there was a crowd watching his every move. Always good for the ego, but little else.

He followed Jason as he walked up the road, thankfully in the right direction, keeping about twenty yards behind. Saturday shoppers were making their way home with overflowing carrier bags. They too looked at his guitar, so Morgan stared at their shopping.

It was about a ten-minute walk to the Royal Concert Hall, at the end of Buchanan Street. Morgan had been to Glasgow only once before, but found he recognized some of the streets, although new buildings were still being built. He kept his eye on Jason's back as he dodged in and out of shoppers, and then saw him enter the large modern concert hall up ahead.

Morgan jogged to catch up, pushed open the front doors and saw Jason asking directions from an usher. There were quite a few people milling about in the lobby, as if some event had been going on earlier. Then Morgan remembered that this concert was part of the Country Connections Festival, which had already been going on for several days. So he kept his distance just to be safe, and only caught up with Jason once he had entered the concert hall itself.

It was a large venue, with a capacity of fourteen hundred according to Jason's tour details, dark blue seats downstairs, and more upstairs in the circle. Morgan couldn't imagine what performing in front of such a crowd would be like. The only audience he had ever stood before was about twenty coppers in an incident room at a murder inquiry.

Jason was talking to a couple of men in jeans who stood next to what Morgan presumed was a sound desk. Lots of knobs and switches. Why on earth did they need so many? Morgan had about ten knobs on his stereo, and found most of those surplus to requirements. On the stage he could see three musicians clearing away their instruments. He looked more closely to see if one of them was Calista Shaw, but no such luck.

'I'm going to do my soundcheck now,' Jason said when he walked over. 'Shouldn't take too long. Do you want to stay here?'

'I may as well see how it all happens. Do you get a dressing room?'

'Yeah. They'll show me to that afterwards. They're going to feed us as well. I told them you were my manager.'

'Fair enough. What shall I say if they ask me something technical?'

'Just act like an arrogant bastard and say you're only in it for the money. You'll fit right in.'

Morgan followed Jason towards the stage. The three musicians had now disappeared and Jason climbed up and opened his guitar case. Morgan set the other one on the stage and sat a few rows back in the auditorium.

The soundcheck only took about fifteen minutes. First Jason plugged in his guitar and strummed without singing, while the technicians got the guitar sound just right. Then he started singing along to his playing, an old Johnny Cash song that Morgan recognized, and a few minutes later it was all over. Morgan was impressed with how good it all sounded through a proper PA in a big hall. He rarely went to concerts himself, so the only live music he ever caught was in local pubs, rock bands thrashing away, where decibel level seemed more important than quality. He was looking forward to seeing Calista Shaw performing in such an arena.

The stage manager was a big, red-faced man called Michael, and he led them off the stage and behind the scenes. It was a confusing maze of corridors, and their dressing room was about the size of Morgan's living room, and the furniture looked more expensive: a coffee table, a full-length mirror near the door, two dark blue sofas, and plenty of matching armchairs.

'Very nice,' Morgan said, when Michael had disappeared. 'Have you ever had a dressing room as big as this?'

'I've never had a dressing room,' Jason said, with a big smile on his face. 'I've only played piddly little clubs, remember.'

Then he disappeared to check out the bathroom. When he came back out he said, 'Take a look in there.'

Morgan walked through to take a look. The bathroom was larger than his own as well, and apart from the toilet had two clean shower stalls, with white towels all laid out. The star treatment. He went back to the dressing room and said, 'I think I'll move in.'

Jason started unpacking his guitars. Morgan sat on a sofa and watched. 'Do you start getting nervous now, or just before you go on?' he asked.

'I haven't felt nerves for quite a while,' Jason said. 'Just a mild feeling of excitement. But that's because I don't play very big places. I don't know how I'll feel tonight. It'll be a new experience. I feel OK at the moment, though.'

When Jason was happy with things, they caught a lift down to another level and walked along a corridor to the staff canteen. Morgan looked at his watch. Six-fifteen. He wondered if the stalker was in Glasgow yet.

In the canteen Jason tucked into his chicken, vegetables and potatoes while watching Jesse Morgan eat some spicy chicken on rice. Food was something Jason had to be careful about, and rice was a no-no for a start, with too many small pieces that might regurgitate and stick in the throat mid-song. Dairy products were out, too; they made a thick saliva form at the back of the throat. He also needed time to digest. He would never eat if it were under an hour until stage time.

'Good food?' Morgan asked.

'Yeah. Tasty enough. Even tastier when it's free. Keeps my bills down.'

'So how much do you think you'll clear overall?'

'It's hard to tell. I get paid a hundred pounds a night, less expenses. So I might only be clearing fifty pounds a time. If I can find people to stay with it'll help.'

'How will you do that?'

'I'll announce it from the stage.'

'You're kidding!'

'No. I've done it before. When I was younger I used to play quite a long way from home. If I'd been drinking too much or couldn't be bothered driving home, I'd announce during the set that I needed somewhere to crash out. It worked quite well a few times. You'd be surprised how many lonely young ladies are out there.'

Morgan smiled. 'Was that part of the bargain? Sex for a bed?'

'Not always. But I had to keep an open mind.'

'But you couldn't do that at a big concert, could you?'

Jason speared a piece of chicken. 'No. Only in smaller places. And there are plenty of those coming up.'

'So you intend doing it on this tour?'

'It's the only way I'll make a decent profit.'

'Well, you won't catch me sleeping on someone's floor.'

'You won't have to. You'll be tucked up in some hotel, all expenses paid.'

'It could work, but it might be risky. You'll have to keep me well informed. I carry the can if something goes wrong.'

'I'll get the addresses first.'

'Make sure you do.' Morgan took a sip of water. 'So how much does Calista get per night?'

'She'll be getting anywhere between a thousand and three thousand, I imagine.'

'Wow. Nice work if you can get it.'

'Well, they deserve it. Most of them have been struggling for years. Plus she may not be in the limelight long. She has to get it while she can.'

'And does she pay her road manager out of that?'

'Yeah, and her expenses, although her record company may chip in for some of those. What happens is, she'll get a guaranteed minimum for each venue; the bigger the venue, the bigger the guarantee. Then, if there's anything left over after the promoter's paid all his expenses, she'll get, say, eighty-five per cent of that. So in these big halls, if they're full, the artist can make a killing.'

Morgan stabbed a piece of spicy chicken with his fork. 'Let's hope we don't see any killing tonight.'

They finished their meal, then wandered around the various lobbies for a while. There was a gift shop, where Morgan bought a Celtic cross for his old girlfriend, and a CD stand where Jason hardly recognized any of the acts on sale. He would've liked to have brought some of his own tapes to sell, but they would have been too heavy to carry. Maybe down south he could take some along.

The concert was due to start at seven-thirty, with the trio they had seen earlier who were called Flook. Jason was due on at eight for thirty minutes.

At seven-fifteen he told Morgan he was going back to the dressing room to get tuned and warmed up.

'You'll be all right on your own?' Morgan asked.

'I'll be fine. I'm convincing myself the stalker won't be here yet.'

'I don't think he will be either. Well, good luck. I'm going to the box office to pick up my free ticket. I'll see you in the upstairs bar at the interval.'

Jason said goodbye and went through a door that led backstage. When he was in the dressing room he tuned his guitar to concert pitch, and then did some singing exercises. He wasn't feeling nervous at all, and was a bit worried about it. He should be feeling more nervous than this, more pumped up. He stood in front of the full-length mirror and strummed through a few songs. He would be singing standing up for the whole tour, which would make a nice change from the crummy Mojo stage where he always had to sit because it had such a low ceiling. Hardly any American performers seemed to sit, and Jason would follow suit.

At a quarter to eight, there was a knock on the door and Michael the stage manager came in.

'Fifteen minutes to showtime,' he said. 'And this just came in for you.' He had a folded piece of paper in his hand and passed it over.

'What is it?' Jason asked.

'A telephone message left at the box office. Can you be at the stage entrance in ten minutes?'

'Sure,' Jason said, looking at the piece of paper. He didn't have a clue who it could be from. He unfolded it, and written there was, 'Good luck tonight. The ghost of Gator will catch you later.'

Jason felt his legs go weak and he collapsed on one of the sofas.

12

Jesse Morgan was quite pleased with his free ticket, although he had to crick his neck to the right to get a good view of the stage; he was sitting at right angles to it, on a slightly higher level than the main auditorium.

The opening act, Flook, had been quite lively; bluegrass instrumentals with the occasional vocal. Morgan had never really been keen on instrumentals, so most of it he sat through without taking it in. He was looking forward to seeing Jason, though. He seemed a decent enough bloke, and they got on fairly well, although neither of them was the biggest conversationalist in the world. Both of them lapsed into long silences now and again, but that was OK. Morgan hated people who felt they had to fill every minute with mindless babble.

Jason came on stage a little late, at five minutes past eight, introduced by Michael. All he said was, 'Ladies and gentlemen, please welcome Jason Campbell.'

Jason came on with his Martin guitar, not the black Takamine Morgan had been carrying, and walked up to the microphone in the middle of the stage. Without saying anything to the audience, he launched into his first song, a slow, moving number which Morgan presumed was called 'The TV And Me', all about living alone when your loved one has left you. It went down well enough, but Jason's voice sounded nervous to Morgan, wavering a bit on the long notes. Jason tried introducing his next song, but his voice was really shaking. Morgan could see something was wrong, and felt very nervous for him. Jason gave up with the talking and launched into an up-tempo number called 'Public Lives' instead. The speed of the song seemed to cover up any singing flaws, and it went down well with the audience.

There was no talking before the third song, a country ballad about drinking called 'A Whisky For The Road'. Morgan was impressed with the lyrics, and wondered if Jason had a drinking problem as well. Morgan hadn't had a drink himself now for five days and felt a lot better for it, but the lyrics of this one almost made him *want* to have a drink. It reminded him of the times he would lose himself in a bottle of whisky; fun times, which unfortunately played havoc with his body, and later, his mind.

That song went down well too, and although Jason was obviously struggling with nerves he was still managing to hold the performance together. Morgan couldn't help but feel admiration for him.

The next song was a slow love ballad called 'Seven Tears' that Jason fingerpicked nicely. He introduced this one briefly, but gave the impression he just wanted to do his songs and get off. The last song didn't get an introduction either. Jason just started strumming, and although he seemed to sing it with passion there were still some nerves showing through. It brought it home to Morgan just how hard it must be to perform in front of so many people.

Jason thanked the audience and walked off stage as quickly as possible, hardly acknowledging the applause.

Morgan left his seat quickly, climbed the staircase to the upstairs bar and caught the lift to the dressing-room level. When he walked inside, Jason was sitting on the sofa with his head in his hands. He looked extremely distressed. Morgan knelt down beside him. 'What's wrong? You look like you've seen a ghost.'

Jason looked up and his face was a mask of anguish. 'You don't know how right you are,' he said. He pointed at a piece of paper on the coffee table. 'I got that just before I went on.'

Morgan picked it up and read it. 'Shit,' he said, and sat down on the sofa too.

They talked it over for twenty minutes or so, and Jason found himself relaxing now that Morgan's reassuring presence was back. Morgan's argument was that they could relax for the moment because the note obviously meant that the stalker wasn't in town. A small consolation, because he was probably on his way.

'I figured that out for myself,' Jason said. 'Just before I went on stage I tried getting it into my head. It made me relax a little, but I was still a bundle of nerves. I couldn't contemplate a sixth song. Five was all I could do. I don't care if they pay me or not.'

'You looked nervous all right, but you sang the songs OK. They were good songs.'

'Thanks.' Jason always knew when he'd performed badly, and that Morgan was just being polite. He felt ashamed of himself. He just wanted to disappear and go back to the hotel; have a shower and a good night's sleep. Prepare for tomorrow's gig in Aberdeen. But would the stalker have caught up with them by then?

'The main question now is,' Morgan continued, 'do you want to carry on with the tour? We have to presume the stalker will catch up with us soon. Do we face him here, or go back to Woodvale and catch him on home ground?'

'I'm not going to cancel the tour,' Jason said. He felt the anger boiling up inside. 'This is my big chance, and I'm not going to let some psycho ruin it. The sooner we catch him the better, anyway. If we go back to Woodvale we may be waiting weeks for him to turn up again.'

'That's a valid point. It's just that there are more coppers in Woodvale. Out here, there's just me.'

'I have every faith in you.'

'Cheers. But I'm unarmed. I don't have a single weapon on me.'

Jason was surprised. 'Not even a gun?'

'This isn't America, you know. We still have our traditional ways.'

'Can't you arrange to get one? I thought you just had to sign a piece of paper or something.'

Morgan shook his head. 'There are only a limited number of officers authorized to carry weapons, and I'm not one of them. I've always been against weapons, so I've never taken the required training.'

'Great. Well, I don't know, I still don't want to cancel the tour. I'll feel OK if you're around. I'd rather you travelled right with me, though, instead of from a distance.'

'OK. That can be done. I'll just pretend I'm your manager, as you suggested.'

They sat in silence for a while and then Jason started clearing up his gear. 'I really don't want to stay for the rest of the concert,' he said. 'I know you want to see Calista, but I just want to go back to the hotel.'

Morgan held up his hands. 'That's fine with me. Whatever you want. I've got the whole tour to see Calista. Have you met her yet?'

'Haven't seen her at all. I saw her tour manager, though. Some big American bloke.'

'Maybe we'll meet her tomorrow.'

They left the dressing room and Jason followed Morgan to the stage door. They could hear Calista Shaw on stage, her soaring voice singing along to an acoustic guitar. Jason didn't even know if she was appearing alone on stage each night, or if someone was backing her. The stage manager Michael was there, sitting at a small table eating a steak.

'I'm glad to see someone is still eating beef,' Morgan said to him.

'Can't beat a good steak,' Michael said.

Jason thought he looked unhealthy. His skin was too red and he was overweight. If that was an advertisement for steak-eating, he wasn't interested.

'Where do we go for Jason's money?' Morgan asked. 'We're about to leave.'

'Just wait here,' Michael said. He picked a mobile phone off the desk and made a call. A few minutes later a young lady came down with an invoice book and a cheque. Jason signed his name and thought they'd got it wrong when he saw the amount on the cheque.

'This is for two hundred pounds,' he said. 'Shouldn't it be a hundred?'

'Two hundred was the agreement with your agent,' the lady said. 'I wouldn't complain about it.'

She left them standing there, and the extra amount helped to lift some of Jason's bad feelings. He also felt extra guilty, though, because of his poor performance.

'A nice little earner,' Morgan said, patting him on the back. They said goodbye to Michael, who grunted with a mouthful of food, and headed for the nearest Exit sign.

Back in his hotel room, Jesse Morgan picked up his mobile phone and dialled Ian Kiddie's home number. He sat by the window and looked at the view. A brick wall.

They talked for a while about the tour, and then Morgan asked about the Brady murder case.

'It's all a dead end at the moment,' Kiddie said. 'SOCO turned up nothing of any use, no one on the estate saw anything and we haven't found the murder weapon. There might be one lead, though.'

'What's that?'

'Well, we checked out Monica Brady's last husband. The one that was meant to be in jail.'

'I remember.'

'He was released last week after doing seven years for armed robbery, and hasn't been seen since. We contacted his parents in Hastings. They had a postcard from him saying he was out but he hasn't returned home yet.'

'Maybe he wants to live it up first. Most of them do.'

'Could be. Probably can't live it up in Hastings.'

Morgan chuckled. 'It does sound a bit fishy, though.'

'So I went to see Monica Brady again, and she hadn't heard from him either, although she didn't particularly want to hear from him. I asked if there was any long-standing feud between her ex and Brady, and she said she couldn't think of anything. So to all intents and purposes, it's another dead end. But I'd like to know where he is so we can ask him ourselves.'

'We could go to the press. Splash his photo all over the papers. That should flush him out.'

'That's what Cole suggested.'

'Great minds think alike.'

'So that's what we're going to do. Tomorrow morning.'

'Seems like the only way to go at the moment. What was his name again?'

'Peppers.'

'Teddy Peppers. How could I forget?'

'An unusual name.'

'Too right.'

They hung up and Morgan read for a while in bed, a book called *A Joseph Campbell Companion* that Nicola had recommended to him a long time ago but which he had never picked up until now.

Joseph Campbell was a famous philosopher, and the book was subtitled *Reflections on the Art of Living*. Campbell's most famous saying was 'Follow your bliss', which meant you should follow your heart in life, do the things that made you happy, rather than what society decreed you should do. Morgan supposed that he was about to follow his bliss, now that he had chosen to pack in the force, although he still didn't really know what his particular kind of bliss was. Maybe he would find out in the coming months. He chuckled at the thought that he was now on the road with two Campbells.

He stopped reading after half an hour and turned off his

light. He had told Jason to lock himself in his room and not answer the door to anyone. If anything suspicious did happen, he had told him to ring, but Morgan was certain they would be all right for tonight. And probably for Aberdeen tomorrow. If he were the stalker he would wait for the tour to go south a little, save unnecessary travel. But he also knew that nutters didn't always think logically and that he should be prepared for anything.

He lay there and wondered where the stalker was now.

13

Outside on a tree a thrush was having a crap, but it was over in a second. Then it turned and stared at Teddy Peppers, who was looking out through the kitchen window. He gave it the finger and it flew away. He wished *his* craps were as quick as that.

It was a grey Sunday morning and he had left Vivian up in bed sleeping. He would have to get her up in a minute, though, because today was the start of their trip north on the trail of Jason Campbell.

The view from the kitchen window was that of a narrow garden, a wooden fence and then the house next door. Teddy was becoming fond of his new lodgings already. He wondered if there was any way he could come out of this with the house to himself. Or should he shack up with Vivian and tell her the whole story? But then he thought of her age. Seventeen years older than him. When he was forty, she'd be fifty-seven. No, he would have to forget about that plan.

He fixed himself tea and toast, such a luxury in this new life. He lashed on some marmalade nice and thick, and made the tea extra milky. He stood at the window while he ate it, looking with fascination at the bathroom window opposite. Someone was in there having a wash. The opaque glass got in the way, but he was pretty sure it was a woman having a body wash, or a whore's bath, as one of the other criminals used to call them. He could feel his groin beginning to stir, and thought that maybe it was time he woke Vivian up.

He carried a cup of tea upstairs. She was sitting up in bed

waiting for him with a smile on her face. Her eagerness was almost endcaring, but he could see it becoming an irritant after a while. But he would have to go along with it for now. She could come in very useful. She had already proved what an asset she could be by finding out about Campbell's tour, and then having the idea about sending a message. He would've liked to have seen Campbell's face when he got that one. They had specifically asked for him to get it just before he went on stage. He hoped it had ruined his performance.

'You read my mind,' Vivian said as she took the cup of tea.

Like a book, Teddy said to himself. 'That's what I'm here for,' he said out loud. 'To serve and satisfy.'

He opened up his dressing gown, one that her ex-husband had left behind, and showed her what was rising underneath to greet her.

'Yum, yum,' Vivian said. 'A sausage as well.'

A few hours later she watched him from the living-room window as he put their suitcases into the Polo. She had the telephone next to her ear, listening to it ringing at her daughter's house. There was no answer, so she left a message on the answerphone saying she was going away for a week with a nice new man she had met. She said she'd bring him round to tea when they got back. She had to laugh at that. She couldn't imagine Teddy having tea with anyone.

There was something scary about Teddy, but she found that quite appealing. He was physically strong and in very good shape. His body was hard all over as if he worked out regularly, and his penis got rock hard when they were making love. There were different levels of hardness in a man's penis: if he was just going through the motions, it could be erect to the sight but not to the touch; if he really wanted it bad it would be extra hard and would take a long time to shrink afterwards. Vivian was glad she had a rock-hard one now after her last few lovers, who had been men her age or older, and were really way past their best. And didn't want to admit it either.

Teddy came back up the driveway looking furtively around. He never seemed to relax unless he had a few drinks inside him, and his eyes darted all over the place, constantly on edge. She would try to give him a massage later, and tell him to slow down. If she could change him in a few ways, their relationship might have possibilities. She liked the idea of having a toyboy. He could be her Teddy boy.

'Ready to go?' he asked, poking his head around the door.

'Ready to go,' she said.

'Got your handbag?'

'Got my handbag.'

'Got your door key?'

'Got my door key.'

'Got your credit cards?'

'Got my credit cards.'

She didn't know why he'd asked that last question, but who cared? She walked past him as he held open the door.

'So,' Jesse Morgan asked, 'do you know any corny country music titles?'

They were on the train to Aberdeen, a three-hour journey. He watched Jason think about it.

'The obvious one is "Drop Kick Me Jesus Through The Goalposts Of Life",' Jason said.

Morgan smiled. 'Heard it. How about "I'm Just A Bug On The Windshield Of Life"?'

Jason nodded. 'A terrible one. How about "My Wife Ran Off With My Best Friend And I Sure Do Miss Him"?'

Morgan chuckled. 'I think so. Here's one I hadn't heard until recently: "I Don't Know Whether To Kill Myself Or Just Go Bowling".'

Jason laughed. 'A good one. Do you think there really are songs with these titles? Or do people just make them up?'

'I reckon they're just made up.'

'I don't know. There could be songs on some stupid album somewhere. How about "When You Leave, Walk Out Backwards So I'll Think You're Walking In"?'

'Yeah, heard that one. "If You Leave Me Can I Come Too?"'

'"I Changed Her Oil, She Changed My Life."'

'Haven't heard that one. "You Can't Have Your Kate And Edith Too".'

Jason cringed. 'That's terrible. That has to be made up. I actually saw a song called "Pubic Hair" on an album once. That was some Canadian singer, though.'

Morgan laughed. 'Not the sort of song that would pass the Nashville test. I saw one called "Puke On the Yukon".'

'This could go on for ever. Have you heard of Kinky Friedman?'

'No.'

'He's a Texan singer-songwriter. If you want amusing songs, he's your man. Writes some good straight songs as well.'

'I'll check him out,' Morgan said. 'How about "If The Phone Don't Ring Baby, You'll Know It's Me"?'

Jason held up a hand. 'No more, please!'

Morgan was glad to see Jason lightening up after the traumas of last night. If it took country music titles to make him laugh, then he'd have to remember some more.

He was sitting next to the aisle, and he watched two jovial Scottish businessmen a few seats down drinking all the way. They were red-faced, in their fifties, and the miniatures of gin were piling up in front of them. The young man pushing the drinks trolley up and down the train had to make special trips to keep them refilled. The businessmen tried joking with him, but he didn't seem to have much of a sense of humour. Too young and serious. Morgan envied the men. He would like to be knocking a few strong ones back as well. The passing scenery deserved the relaxed eye of the mellow drunk. But he was now on his sixth drinkless day. There was no point in ruining the sequence.

At Aberdeen they unloaded their suitcases and guitars and joined a long taxi queue. Morgan looked at the surrounding buildings and said nonchalantly, 'Welcome to the Silver City.'

'The what?' Jason asked.

'The Silver City,' Morgan said, trying to impress. 'So called because the granite from which most of the buildings are built glistens silver in the sun.'

'I suppose you got that from your travel book,' Jason said.

Morgan nodded, feeling caught out. 'It's full of interesting information.'

'It looks like any other grey city to me,' Jason said. 'Any other nuggets for me?'

'It's also called the Houston of the north, because of the oil industry. It's also a fishing port.'

'Maybe you could work on a travel programme when you retire,' Jason said. Morgan gave him a wry smile.

When it was finally their turn in the queue they took a short ride to the next venue, a small club called the Lemon Tree. Morgan could see Jason visibly relax as soon as they walked in. It was a smallish club with a bar on the right, and their information sheets said it held three hundred.

'This is more my kind of scene,' Jason said. 'Fucking concert halls. Who needs them?'

They were introduced to the manager of the club, a large woman called Madge. Then a young guy with a bald head came over and shook their hands.

'My name's Neil Brickhouse,' he said. 'I'm with PMA. I'll be doing the rest of the tour with you. How was last night?'

Morgan didn't know who PMA were. He presumed they were the tour's promoters, but he'd find out later. As for PMA, what did that stand for? Positive Mental Attitude?

'Large and impersonal,' Jason said. 'I'd rather play places like this.'

'It's a good venue,' Neil said. 'It's a sell-out as well. And it's an attentive audience. Would you like a coffee?'

He led them to a coffee machine at the bar and told them to help themselves. Morgan eyed the place over. There were a few members of staff carrying chairs around, placing them in rows facing the stage. A few other people sat at tables, drinking, and there was a jovial old guy in a raincoat wandering around as if he were lost. No obvious sign of the stalker.

Neil took them upstairs to what would be their dressing room. It wasn't a dressing room as such, just an empty storage room. There was a table with four chairs around it and a few stacks of chairs waiting to go downstairs. It was back to reality after last night's luxury.

'Just dump your stuff in here,' Neil said. 'Soundcheck should be around five-thirty. Calista Shaw is on her way, apparently. We'll do her first.'

Morgan felt a flutter in his stomach. At last he would meet the great lady.

Jason slumped into a chair. 'I think I'll take a nap,' he said.

'In a chair?' Morgan said.

'I'll make it to the floor in a minute. Can you wake me for the soundcheck?'

'Sure. I'll go downstairs and meet Calista.'

The journey up north for Teddy and Vivian began on the M25, which was only a mile away from Vivian's house. Once they were on that, they headed west and all the way round until they reached the M1.

Vivian insisted on trying to educate Teddy by playing him a Richard Clayderman tape, but it was more than Teddy could stand, so at the first service station he went inside to see what he could buy to retaliate with. He didn't recognize half the names that sat in front of him on the small cassette rack, so he bought one by Meatloaf and another by a ska group called Mistakes, which the man behind the counter recommended. Teddy didn't even know what ska was, but he had more than a few scars himself, so he bought it.

When they were moving again he played one side of each as they went up the M1, much to Vivian's disapproval. She thought they were both tuneless pieces of rubbish, but Teddy was bopping to them both, especially the ska. When they'd finished, Vivian insisted on *Neil Diamond's Greatest Hits*, so Teddy sulked and flicked through the *Q* magazine they'd bought for the Calista Shaw tour dates. His plan was to head for Preston, which was the fourth date on the schedule after Aberdeen and South Shields. That would save them having to drive the length of Britain. Let the hunted do all the travelling.

Teddy was also trying to figure out a way of getting some more credit cards and cash, and the obvious way was to mug someone in the toilets of a motorway service station. So he made Vivian stop just after they passed Luton, and while she was in the canteen he went to the gents and hung around for five minutes looking for a suitable candidate. The problem was, though, this being a Sunday, all the men were dressed casually, so it was impossible to tell who had some cash on them. He stood at one of the sinks, longing for a suit to make an appearance. Businessmen were so easy to mug because their suits and briefcases announced them as men with dosh. As most of them were overweight and unfit as well, it made them doubly easy to knock over. But today it obviously wasn't going to happen, so he left the toilet and went to find Vivian.

He found her sitting at a table with a cup of tea and a sandwich in a plastic wrapper. She had bought the same for him and he sat down opposite and ate in silence. He watched families at other tables with their noisy kids, still hoping to see a man in a suit.

'What's wrong with you?' Vivian asked. 'Cat got your tongue?'

'Nothing,' Teddy said. He hated that saying. 'Getting tired

of travelling, I suppose. And listening to Neil Diamond and that other twat.' He hated Richard Clayderman so much he couldn't bring himself to say his name.

'You don't know what you're missing,' Vivian said. 'At least they play tunes.'

Teddy grunted and went silent again. There was not much point in winding Vivian up. They still had a long way to travel together.

When they'd finished, Vivian said that she had to get some more money. Teddy followed her to one of the cash machines outside and stood up close as she punched in her numbers. He had never used one of these machines before, so he paid careful attention and remembered everything she did in sequence, especially her personal pin number. He found it fascinating, and his eyes nearly popped out when a hundred pounds in crisp notes slid out of the slot in front of them.

'A hundred pounds, just like that,' he said.

'I can get three hundred a day if I want to,' Vivian replied.

'Could be handy,' Teddy said, but Vivian didn't hear; she was already heading back to the car. He looked at her with a new train of thought going through his head. Suddenly life seemed full of possibilities again.

14

While Jesse Morgan was waiting for Calista Shaw to turn up, he sat at a table at the back of the Lemon Tree and made phone calls to local bed and breakfasts on his mobile. He found a cheap one at twenty-five pounds a night, and they said they had more spare rooms should he need one. Morgan had agreed with Jason that tonight he could try his method of lobbying for free board from the stage. Morgan had major doubts about it working, but it would be good fun to see what happened. If it kept Jason happy then it was worth trying, and if it didn't work, he could just book him into the same B&B.

When Calista Shaw made her entrance at five-thirty, Morgan sat up straighter in his seat to watch. She came in carrying a guitar in a large white case, and walking behind her was a large man also carrying a case. She was wearing a black dress which came to her calves and a waist-length black coat. He wondered if he were seeing things, because she looked totally different from her CD covers. On her CD covers she was portrayed as a glamorous blonde, with high cheekbones and a thin face, but in real life she was overweight, very short and round in the face. Obviously some creative airbrushing had been used on the CD picture.

Morgan left his seat and walked over to the coffee machine to see if he could eavesdrop on her conversation with the Lemon Tree staff. When he'd filled his cup, though, Neil from PMA came over and said, 'Let me introduce you to Calista Shaw.'

Morgan felt nervous as he followed Neil over. He was

introduced as Jason's manager and reached out to shake her hand. She was at least a foot shorter than he was, and she was wearing heels!

'I'm a big fan of yours,' he said, hoping not to sound like an idiot. 'I've got both your CDs.'

'Why thank you,' Calista said. 'Jesse's an unusual name for an Englishman.'

'It was my father,' Morgan said sheepishly. 'He was a big fan of westerns.'

'It's a nice name,' Calista said, and then she turned to the man beside her who was slightly taller than Morgan and at least five stone heavier. 'This is Hoss,' she said. 'His father was a fan of *Bonanza*.'

They all laughed and Morgan shook his hand too.

Then it was time for the soundcheck and Calista climbed on stage. Morgan went back to his seat and watched as she took a black guitar out of one of the cases and plugged it in. Like Jason last night, she strummed her guitar until it sounded right, and then tested her vocals while the sound-man twiddled knobs at a desk just in front of Morgan. When Morgan heard her voice he forgave her that she looked totally different. It was the same poppish voice, clear and sharp, every word easily heard. He recognized the song she was playing and searched his memory for the title. It was called 'Every Man I Can', about a mother struggling to make ends meet for her kid, so she goes out and becomes a prostitute. Morgan had met a few of those in his time, and thought the sentiments of the song were spot on.

She sang bits of other songs to make sure the vocals were just right, and then tested the second guitar. When she was finished she left both guitars sitting on stage on a couple of stands. She smiled a lot and seemed a nice woman, but Morgan was then horrified to see her puffing on a cigarette that Hoss offered her. Weren't all singers meant to be non-smokers? Her voice didn't sound like a smoker's voice.

He left his table quickly and walked to the stage before she disappeared. He stopped her as she stepped carefully down in her heels, and held up his CD.

'Could I get you to sign this before you go?' he asked.

'Sure, Jesse,' she said. 'Do you have a pen, Hoss?'

Hoss produced a felt tip from the back pocket of his jeans. He looked like he could have just stepped off a ranch somewhere. His skin was weather-beaten and tanned, and his nose was bulbous and twisted. In his big hands the pen looked like a pin. A cigarette dangled from his mouth.

Morgan watched like a little kid as she removed the CD cover and wrote something on it. She handed it back and gave him her best Nashville smile. He thanked her and stood back as they made their way out of the door and back to the hotel for a meal.

Feeling chuffed, Morgan walked upstairs to the makeshift dressing room and found Jason asleep on the floor, his head resting on his coat. He shook him by the shoulder and held the CD above his head. 'Look what I've got,' he said. 'A Calista Shaw autograph.'

Jason looked up at him with a sleepy half-smile. 'I'm very happy for you,' he said.

By the time it was dark, Teddy and Vivian were already in Preston, and Teddy was wondering whether they should travel to South Shields tomorrow instead of waiting around for a day for the tour to reach them. He had never travelled this far north in his life, and came to the quick conclusion that he hadn't been missing much. It was drizzling outside as they drove around looking for somewhere to stay, and the streets looked grimy and uninteresting. They found a place called The Byron Lodge Hotel up a street called Grimshaw. Teddy made a joke about it sure being grim, but it was wasted on Vivian.

They parked around the back of the hotel and rang a bell at the locked front door.

'See, it's so grim up here they don't even let you walk in without looking you over first,' Teddy said.

'You can't be too sure these days,' Vivian said, and Teddy turned his collar up against the rain.

A woman opened the door and they followed her through a small lobby into reception.

'We'd like a double room for two nights,' Teddy said, then waited while the woman walked through a door and appeared on the other side of them behind some strong-looking glass in a hatch. She slid the glass back and started filling out forms.

'How would you like to pay?' she asked.

'Diner's card all right?' Teddy said.

The woman looked up. 'That's the only card we don't take.'

Teddy looked at Vivian. 'That's the only card I have on me. I must've left the others at your place.'

Vivian looked at him in disbelief. 'That's all right. I'll pay for this one.' She reached in her handbag and brought out a credit-card holder. 'MasterCard OK?'

'Fine,' said the woman. 'Just as long as I know. You can pay when you check out.'

Vivian put the cards back in her bag and Teddy gave her a big smile. He didn't have a Diner's card at all. It was the only one not listed on the front door's glass.

The woman led them up some narrow stairs to their room. It was small and clean with a double bed and a TV. They dropped their overnight bags on the bed.

When the woman was gone Vivian said, 'Does this mean I'm going to have to pay for everything on this trip?'

'I'll pay you back, I promise,' Teddy said. 'I think I left my wallet in your bedroom. I only discovered I didn't have it when we were past Luton. That's why I was so quiet after that. I felt guilty about it.'

'So you don't even have a Diner's card?'

'I made that up to save an embarrassing scene.'

Vivian shook her head. 'Is there any hope for you? Come here and let me give you a hug.'

Teddy walked obediently to her and into her waiting arms. He bowed his head and nestled against her large breasts and smiled to himself.

Neil Brickhouse told Jason he could have a forty-minute set tonight, which Jason usually reckoned to be about eight songs. The soundcheck had gone well and he was feeling a lot more relaxed than last night. Morgan said he would be downstairs in the audience, sitting close to the stage, waiting for anything unusual to happen. Jason was feeling confident that nothing would.

There was a knock on the dressing-room door at five to eight, and Neil popped his bald head round. 'Are you ready, Jason?'

Neil had a soft Liverpool accent, which Jason hadn't noticed before. 'Ready for action,' he said.

He walked down the stairs carrying his guitar, and then had to wait a few minutes at the bottom for eight o'clock to roll around. He could see into the bar and the place looked packed. Sometimes it was harder to play in bars because if you weren't good enough the audience would just forget you and turn to their drinks and conversation. A few doubts entered Jason's mind, but he quickly brushed them away. Then Neil gave him the nod, wished him good luck and he stepped up into the lights.

Jesse Morgan was sitting in the third row from the front with an orange juice under his chair. He was wishing it were a pint, but that couldn't be helped. He watched Jason come on stage wearing faded blue jeans, black T-shirt and his cowboy boots.

The set went a lot better than the previous night, Jason looking relaxed and talking to the audience. He even made them laugh a few times, and loosened them up halfway

84

through by singing a cover version of an old Cat Stevens song called 'The First Cut Is The Deepest'. Morgan had always thought Rod Stewart wrote it.

When Jason had just one song left he went into a little speech about not having anywhere to stay the night, and that he would be grateful for any offers during the interval. Morgan sat in disbelief, smiling to himself, wondering if anyone would fall for it. He was interested to see what would happen.

When the last song was over there was a good round of applause, and Jason waved to the audience as he walked off. Morgan left his seat and made his way backstage. 'So, do you think that worked?' he asked, when they were in the dressing room.

'We'll soon find out,' Jason said. 'I'd better get down to the bar before Calista comes on.'

'Don't tell them I'm your manager. They'll think I'm a skinflint.'

Back down in the bar, several people came up and asked Jason if he had any tapes to sell. He took their addresses and five pounds off each person, and promised to send them one as soon as he got home. Morgan watched with amusement, wondering if anyone would offer a bed.

Eventually the old guy in the raincoat, who Morgan had noticed when they first arrived at the club, wandered over and introduced himself as Charlie Smillie. He said he had a bed on offer if Jason would like it. Jason started to look worried until the old man waved a good-looking woman over and introduced her as his daughter Pam.

'She's staying the night with me as well,' Charlie said.

That made up Jason's mind for him and he accepted the offer.

'We'll meet you after the show,' Charlie said, and then they went back to their seats.

Morgan shook his head with disbelief. 'You're a jammy sod,' he said.

'I told you it would work,' Jason said. 'That's saved me thirty-odd quid.'

'Well, don't forget to give me the address. I'll pick you up in a taxi in the morning.'

'Fair enough. Now can we find a seat for the show? I still haven't seen Calista Shaw in the flesh.'

'Don't hold your breath,' Morgan said.

15

Now that the money problem was out of the way, Teddy found himself relaxing a bit more with Vivian. It meant he didn't have to go looking for someone to mug, and could just sponge off her for the duration of their trip.

She took him out for a Chinese meal on Sunday night, and Teddy had two cold pints of lager to wash it down. The food tasted great after seven years without, but an hour after they'd finished he felt hungry once again. So Vivian took him to a wine bar where he stuffed two pieces of cheesecake down his throat while they shared a bottle of wine.

Back in The Byron Lodge Hotel they had rough sex, and one of the other residents started banging on the wall in complaint. They fell into a drunken sleep afterwards and didn't wake up until the maid started knocking on their door. Teddy looked at his watch. He wasn't surprised to see they were too late for breakfast.

They showered and dressed, and left the hotel to look for something to eat. They made do with a little café, and Teddy had a full English breakfast while Vivian had cereal and fruit. 'I have to look after myself at my age,' she said. 'I can't eat all that fatty stuff.'

'Live now, pay later,' Teddy said. He almost added that if Vivian had been in jail for seven years, then she too would be stuffing her face at every opportunity.

'That's what my husband said,' Vivian continued, as she spooned a prune into her mouth. 'He smoked, he drank, he had his own business and then he came down with angina.'

'Ann who?' Teddy said, but Vivian didn't laugh.

'He had to cut back his work, give up sex, change his diet and wait for months for the National Health to see him. When they finally got through with his tests he had to go in for an operation. When he'd got over that he decided life was too short to be living it with me, so he moved out and found himself a younger model.'

'Bastard,' Teddy said, trying to summon up some interest. He thought Vivian might burst into tears at any moment.

'An insecure bastard. He sees my daughter once a month now, and that's it. To all intents and purposes we don't exist any more. So the moral of the story is, go easy on all that fatty food, it may change your life.'

Teddy looked down at his greasy bacon and egg and felt guilty for having it in front of him. 'Can I just finish this one meal?' he asked.

Sitting in the taxi next to Jesse Morgan, Jason was paying the price for his free night of accommodation.

'We stayed up till one-thirty drinking malt,' he said, his head pounding like a hammer. 'That Charlie had more energy that I've *ever* had, and he's eighty-three.'

'And what about his daughter?' Morgan asked. 'How much energy did she have?'

'She was pretty quiet, actually. She sat listening to us for most of the evening. She seemed quite shy.'

'And?'

'And nothing. I tried getting her on her own, but you can't make a pass when the father's around. Would've liked to, though. I got her address. She actually lives in Edinburgh. She came up to see the concert and her father.'

'Edinburgh's a long way from Surrey.'

'She comes down to London on business trips. You never know.' But Jason didn't feel as hopeful as he sounded.

The taxi dropped them at Aberdeen station and they carried their luggage and guitars to the platform. Aboard the southbound train they travelled down the east coast of

Scotland, a different route to the journey up, and with the sun shining on the sea it was a pleasant ride. They passed golf courses on the inland side, and on their left small coastal villages, which Morgan told Jason were mainly fishing communities. He had bought a *Daily Mail* at the station and showed Jason a picture of someone called Teddy Peppers.

'This is a man we're looking for at the moment,' he said. 'He may or may not have committed a murder in Redgate. It was meant to be in yesterday's papers, but didn't make it.'

'A mean-looking bloke,' Jason said, taking the newspaper. It was a classic police mugshot, an aggressive face staring hard at the camera, quite good-looking though with short hair. The man was an armed robber, but was wanted in connection with a murder on the Holmethorpe Industrial Estate. A factory worker had been beaten to death with a wooden implement in the small hours of last Wednesday morning. Jason remembered Morgan mentioning it last week at the police station.

'So this is the only lead you have?' Jason asked.

Morgan nodded. 'And a slender one at that. I've a bad feeling about this case. I've got a hunch it's going to slip away from us. Five days without a sniff is not a good sign.'

'Something'll turn up.'

'I hope so. We need a Frankie Bosser to solve it for us.'

Jason tensed at the mention of Frankie. That was a subject he didn't want to talk to Morgan about.

'Still living in Europe, is he?' Morgan asked.

'I don't know,' Jason shrugged. 'We haven't kept in touch. I didn't really know him that well. Our lives just crossed for a few days.' He got the impression Morgan didn't believe him, but he wasn't going to say any more than that. He handed the newspaper back.

After passing through Edinburgh, the train took another one and a half hours to get to Newcastle. Jason had never been there before, and was looking forward to it. He only knew it from the TV series *Crocodile Shoes*, which he had enjoyed, and he had bought several Jimmy Nail CDs because of it. He thought he had a good voice.

Tonight's concert was actually in South Shields, another small venue, this one called the Custom House. They had to catch a metro train from Newcastle to get there, like a tube train except cleaner, and going mainly overground. The passing scenery was mostly industrial.

At the other end they jumped into a taxi and told the driver they needed a B&B somewhere near the venue. Five minutes later he dropped them on a street full of B&Bs that led towards the sea. Jason could see an amusement park at the end of the road, like a mini-Blackpool. Not that he'd ever been to Blackpool.

They stood on the street with their belongings and Morgan said, 'Are you sure you don't want to kip here?'

Jason shook his head. 'No. I'll try my method again. I think I'm on a roll.'

Morgan said, 'Fair enough,' not looking too happy about it.

But Jason was damned if he was going to lose money just because of some nutter who may or may not be following him.

They stepped into the nearest building and Morgan booked a room for one person only.

The Custom House was an attractive venue, a modern building with an excellent restaurant. They sat by a window eating pasta, looking out at the sea. At another table on the far side sat Calista Shaw with Hoss, avoiding all eye contact with them. They had said hello to them at the soundcheck, but Morgan didn't think they'd all be best buddies by the end of the tour.

'It's all very impersonal, isn't it?' he said to Jason.

'What?'

'The tour so far. You turn up in a town, do a soundcheck,

sing for half an hour, then disappear. I thought it would be more fun than this.'

'Like late-night parties and groupies?'

'Something like that.'

'I expected this. Why would she want to mix with us? She's a star and I'm not.'

'Maybe. I just thought country music might be a little friendlier. That's the image it likes to give itself.'

'These people are professionals. I've met a few of them before at the Mojo Club. They'll be friendly to the people they need to be friendly with and blank everyone else. They'll chat to fans and then forget about them. It's all a bit superficial.'

'You're shattering all my illusions.'

'I'm impressed you had any.'

'Being a policeman, you mean?'

'Sorry. That was a bit patronizing.'

Morgan went back to his pasta with pesto sauce. He had been stung by that remark, although it was a regular occurrence. People often thought that because he was a copper he had no feelings or intelligent views on anything. Wrong. He would be glad when it was quitting time, when he would make people treat him like a normal human being.

Later, he sat in the audience and watched Jason sing the same set as the previous night. He talked to the crowd about *Crocodile Shoes* and made them laugh a few times. He was certainly relaxing into the tour. Just before the last song, he once again asked if anyone could put him up for the night. The audience laughed at his audacity, but he got some loud applause as he walked off.

They mingled in the bar afterwards as several people came over to say well done. And sure enough, one of them, a tall man in his thirties, offered Jason a room for the night. He introduced himself as Martyn, Martyn with a Y, and said he was a struggling writer. Morgan gave him the once-over, and signalled to Jason that he looked OK. He was relying on his policeman's instinct, and hoped he was right. It was annoying taking these extra risks, but if that was the way Jason wanted it, he would have to go along with it for now.

Another drawback to this method of accommodation was that they both had to hang around until the end of the show. Neither of them wanted to see the concert again, so they stepped outside and took a walk along the waterfront. The air was fresh with a light fog in it, and they watched a large vessel coming slowly into dock in the distance. Morgan could see that Jason was feeling pretty pleased with himself, on a high from the performance, and feeling smart because he'd found somewhere to sleep again. He asked Morgan about his set, analysing it and reliving it. Morgan humoured him and encouraged him, nurturing his ego, and pitied anyone who had to live with a musician. They leaned on a railing looking out to sea.

'So far so good,' Jason said. 'Maybe touring is the life for me.'

16

Tuesday in Preston was a dull, drizzly day and Teddy was getting tired of hanging around, waiting for the evening. Yesterday they had bought two tickets for tonight's Calista Shaw concert, and Teddy planned to kill Jason Campbell by whatever means it took, so he could leave this dreadful town and go somewhere with a bit more action. Vivian still thought he was just visiting an old friend, but she wouldn't believe that story for ever. He would have to make a move before she became suspicious.

So he humoured her throughout the day, trying to make out how excited he was to be seeing his old buddy once again. She suggested they go to the Harris museum and art gallery to kill time, and Teddy reluctantly agreed. He trudged around in her path for a couple of hours as she oohed and aahed at Bronze Age burial urns, Viking coins and twentieth-century British paintings. Vivian told him that Preston was a busy industrial town, formerly an important port, but to him it was just a tip. And the walking was tiring him out, too.

In the early evening they had a Thai meal, which perked up his mood, and then walked towards the Charter Theatre which was only about five minutes from their hotel. Teddy hadn't drunk any alcohol with his meal, preferring to keep a clear head, and the excuse he gave to Vivian was that he was feeling a bit rough from their constant boozing. She believed him, and still managed to down a whole bottle of white wine herself.

At the theatre, they made their way to their seats which

were in the fourth row from the front. Teddy felt the Beretta in his inside jacket pocket pressing against his chest. It would be a good laugh just to pop Campbell while he was on stage, but escaping would be a bit difficult. A better plan would be to catch him at the stage door when he left. Teddy also had the flick knife strapped to his ankle again, and that might be the better option. A nice quick slit across the throat.

Vivian had bought a packet of crisps and was stuffing them into her mouth. She offered them to Teddy but he declined. He couldn't believe how excited he was at the thought of a little bit of action.

After fifteen minutes of listening to Vivian munching, the house lights dimmed and a voice came over the PA: 'Ladies and gentlemen. Please welcome Calista Shaw's special guest, Jason Campbell.'

There was polite applause, and Teddy smiled at Vivian. She squeezed his arm and smiled back, remnants of the crisps on the front of her blue dress.

He watched Campbell walking on stage, a smug smile on his face, a guitar slung around his neck. Teddy had never seen him this close, and he took in all the details. He looked to be about five-ten, average build, easy to take. He was dressed in jeans and a green T-shirt, and a nice pair of cowboy boots. Teddy had left his at the hotel, and was wearing a pair of trainers instead. He needed to be fleet of foot if he was to be involved in a scrap.

Teddy couldn't concentrate on the music Campbell played, although it was tuneful enough if you liked that sort of thing, but he thought the words were soppy and self-pitying. He thought Campbell could do with a few years in jail to toughen him up. The first song went down well with the audience, though, and so did the one after. He was going down well with Vivian too, who was clapping enthusiastically and even whooped one time. Teddy had to act as if he were enthusiastic as well, but his insides were churning with anger, for this was the man who had helped to kill his old friend Phil Gator. But tonight would be the end of the road for Campbell. Teddy was one hundred per cent sure of that.

The set seemed to go on and on, and Teddy started to sweat. He really wanted to get down to the nitty-gritty, but then his ears perked up and he couldn't believe what he was hearing. Campbell was asking the audience if there was anyone who could put him up for the night! Teddy nearly put his hand up and said, Yes, me please!

He couldn't believe how easy this was panning out. It would be like swatting a fly. That was one of the things he liked about crime. No matter how much you planned something, there was always the unexpected. Sometimes it worked against you, and sometimes it worked in your favour.

Vivian felt Teddy's hand gripping her round the arm as they made their way into the foyer. He seemed excited about something.

'I've just had a great idea,' he said in a forced whisper. He backed her against the wall while the audience squeezed into the bar. Vivian fancied another drink as well. 'Why don't you offer to put Jason up for the night, and bring him back to our hotel? I'll surprise him when you bring him into our room.'

Vivian thought that was a bit over the top, but with the eagerness on Teddy's face, how could she refuse? She also felt a little wary of him. There was a hard edge coming out of him now. Was he really telling her the whole truth about Jason? 'You want me to bring him back to the hotel? Is he going to stay the night with us as well?'

'No, we'll find an empty room for him. I'll go and get some bottles and we'll have a surprise party. How does that sound?'

'What about the concert?'

95

'I'm not bothered about that. I just want to see Jason. You can stay for the show, and then bring him with you. I'll be waiting.'

Vivian let out a deep breath. 'What if he doesn't want to come back with me?'

'You'll just have to persuade him. And here's your chance.'

Jason walked right by them and into the bar. A big man with a beard who Vivian thought was extremely handsome followed him. They seemed to be together. Maybe she could invite them both, and while Teddy and Jason were catching up on old times . . .

'OK,' she said. 'I'll try my best.'

She smoothed down her dress and brushed away the crisp crumbs. Then she walked over to Jason and tapped him on the shoulder.

Morgan saw the woman coming, plumpish and in her fifties, and saw a young man standing over by the wall watching her. He was wearing a black leather jacket and had short dark hair. Morgan felt the hairs on the back of his neck stand up, and that sixth sense told him to beware.

He listened to the woman as she complimented Jason and then offered him a bed for the night. She kept looking at Morgan as well, giving him the eye. When Jason introduced him as his manager she said, 'Would you like to come too?'

Morgan laughed. He could tell the woman was slightly drunk. 'No. I've got a hotel. Jason's the desperate one.' He didn't mean it to come out like that, and the woman looked hurt. 'But maybe I'll come back for a drink. Help you to tuck him in.'

'That would be nice,' the woman smiled. She told them her name was Vivian.

Jason was looking a bit worried, as if this woman wasn't exactly who he had in mind for the night. He had been lucky so far. He'd had another trouble-free evening last night, although the writer called Martyn had wanted to stay up until the early hours talking about football, a subject that didn't interest Jason at all. It was just as well that there was a break in the tour after tonight because at this pace Morgan couldn't see Jason lasting, although he had caught up on his sleep on the train ride to Preston. But maybe one bad night would put him off his crazy way of scrounging bed and board.

'What street do you live in?' Morgan asked. 'Is it near here?'

The woman seemed flustered for a second. 'Grimley Street. The street's called Grimley.'

'OK,' Morgan said. 'It has to be near so we can get an early start.'

'It's only five minutes. About as near as you can get, really.'

'OK. We'll meet you right here when the show's over.'

Vivian seemed genuinely pleased, thanked them both and then hurried back towards the theatre as the bell went for the restart.

Jason raised his eyebrows when she was gone and said, 'You've got to be joking.'

'I think you're in there,' Morgan teased, then left him at the bar.

He walked over to a quiet corner and took the mobile phone out of his pocket. He rang the local police station, told them who he was and asked if Grimley Street existed. A minute later he was told that it didn't. There was a Grimshaw, but not a Grimley.

Morgan knew his sixth sense had been right.

17

They were waiting for her exactly where they said they would, Jason the singer and Jesse the manager. Vivian felt relieved because Teddy would be pleased with her now. At last he could see his old friend, and then tomorrow they could get out of this grimy town to somewhere a bit more interesting. Like the Lake District, maybe, or the Yorkshire moors. But could she really imagine Teddy looking at scenery?

She had enjoyed the Calista Shaw concert. Some of the songs had been a bit too serious for her, but they were all very tuneful and Calista had a lovely voice. One of the songs, about a man changing his life after a heart attack, leaving a wife who he'd never really loved, had been a bit too close to home. What had that one been called? Something like 'You Took The Heart Right Out Of Me'. Maybe she would search out one of her CDs.

'A good concert?' It was Jesse asking her the question, a friendly smile on his face.

'She was very good,' Vivian said. 'I'd never even heard of her until a few days ago.'

'Taking pot luck?'

'Sort of,' Vivian said, knowing she'd better be careful not to give the game away.

She led them on to the main road, a fine drizzle still falling, and they turned left. The two men were carrying a guitar each and Jason had a heavy sports bag over his shoulder. He was being very quiet, though. Quiet as a mouse. Still, it was Jesse she was interested in. He seemed talkative enough. She wouldn't mind ending up in bed with him tonight.

Jason walked along behind, watching Jesse Morgan chatting to the plump woman who he wanted nothing to do with at all. Especially after Morgan had told him about his phone call. There was no such street as Grimley, so where the fuck were they being taken?

Morgan had warned him that this may well be confrontation time, the face-off with the stalker, and they could get it all over with right now, then carry on with the tour in peace. But all Morgan had with him were a pair of handcuffs and his fists. He hadn't even rung for any back-up, just in case Vivian was genuine. Great, Jason thought. What if the stalker was armed with a gun? What chance would they have then? But he walked on behind, having to place his faith in the big man. How on earth could Morgan remain so cool, and keep talking to that horrible woman?

Morgan wished the woman would speed up a bit, because the drizzle was beginning to irritate him. The guitar case was getting a bit shiny and so was his hair. A cold was the last thing he needed.

The name of the street they were on was Church; a few pubs were still open, a few small restaurants. Then he spotted the name Grimshaw on a small side street on the right, and knew this would be the one. The woman had got the name of the street wrong in her desperation to get them to stay with her. So had someone else sent her over to talk to them? Like, maybe, that young man he'd briefly seen looking at them?

Sure enough, they turned down Grimshaw. There was nothing much there, just a takeaway pizza place on the right and then a small hotel a bit farther up on the left.

'Is that where you're staying?' Morgan asked Vivian, pointing ahead.

'Yes, but I've got a spare bed. There's plenty of room.'

Morgan knew by the worried look on her face that this was it. They were being set up, and he'd better be careful.

Vivian reached in her handbag for the front-door key to the hotel. Her hand was shaking. She had never deliberately lied to anyone before, and she hoped these two wouldn't be mad with her. What if Jason didn't want to see Teddy again? What if Teddy had been imagining the whole friendship, and they weren't really that pally at all? But it was too late now. She had played her part and there was no going back.

She had trouble getting the key in the lock, and then found Jesse's big hand wrapped around hers, helping.

'Anything wrong?' he asked, and there was a different tone to his voice, like maybe he knew something was up.

'No, no,' Vivian said. 'Just a bit cold from the rain.'

He seemed to believe that, and the door came open and they went inside.

The foyer of the hotel was just about big enough to swing a cat, and it had a large mirror covering most of the wall on the right. Jason caught his reflection as he stepped in and he looked a little stressed out. He felt more than a little nervous, and just wanted to leave the place behind and stay the night at Morgan's hotel. But no, Morgan seemed to want to go through with it, perhaps teaching him a lesson not to sleep at strangers' houses any more.

Now Vivian was holding a pudgy finger up to her lips, asking them to be quiet. Then she opened a glass door that led to some narrow, carpeted stairs. They followed up behind her, Jason making sure he was last.

They came to a small landing, a few rooms ahead of them, but turned right through another glass door, then left down a short corridor with more rooms. They were all being very quiet, as if they wanted to surprise someone. Jason felt extremely spooked.

They were heading for the door at the end, and just before they got there Morgan turned to Jason and held up a big hand telling him to stop. Vivian hadn't seen the signal, and so Jason obediently stopped walking. He put the guitar case and sports bag on the carpet, and bent down as if to tie a shoelace.

Jesse Morgan was getting interested in this, and was quite keen to see who was on the other side of the door. He watched as Vivian once again struggled with her key but didn't help her this time. He tensed himself, waiting for a possible struggle with whoever was on the other side.

The door clicked open, and lying on the double bed immediately in front of them was the young man Morgan had seen earlier at the concert. The black leather jacket was now gone, and he was lying there in black jeans, black T-shirt and white trainers. Up close the man looked familiar, but Morgan couldn't place him. The man looked very surprised to see him, but before anyone could say a word his hand was rising from beneath a pillow with a gun attached to it.

Morgan tried to back out of the door, but the man started shooting straight away, rapid fire that hit him before he could do anything. He felt sharp pains all over his body, and then he was falling towards the floor on top of Vivian, who had also been hit.

Jason heard gunshots and screams just as he was rising from tying the shoelace that didn't exist – he was still wearing his cowboy boots. Then a stray bullet whizzed past his head and shattered a glass door behind him. Jason decided it was time to leave.

He left his belongings where they were and turned and ran down the stairs. He reached the foyer, opened the front door and jumped into the street.

He ran back the way they'd come, not knowing where to

go, wishing he were in flat-soled shoes so he could run a bit faster. He felt like he might twist an ankle at any moment, but it was surprising how fast you could run with a little fear pushing you along. He ran past groups of people who glared at him, past pubs that were spilling people out of the doors, and then thought that the only safe place to go was back to the concert hall. There would still be people there. It always took ages for the soundmen to clear up. Someone could help him and call the police.

When the two bodies fell at the foot of the bed, Teddy Peppers jumped up and grabbed the important things, like his sports bag, his black leather jacket and Vivian's handbag. He dropped the Beretta quickly into the bag.

He stepped over the bodies and into the corridor where people were starting to gather.

'Call the police!' he shouted at them. 'Someone just shot my friends!'

He walked past them towards the emergency exit that he knew led to the small car park at the back. No one tried to stop him.

He ran down some iron stairs in the dark and drizzle, and marched towards Vivian's car. He jumped in the driver's seat and drove on to Grimshaw Street, then left, away from the main road. He couldn't hear any sirens yet. He had been too quick for them.

His heart was pounding like a bass drum, and he was feeling as high as a kite. He had never shot two people before. What a kick that had been! He wondered who the man with the beard was, and why hadn't Jason Campbell been there? It was all a bit confusing. He would think about it later. Right now he just wanted to put some miles between himself and Preston. Lovely Preston. That was one town he never wanted to see again.

18

Jason sat in the security guard's office, which was by the stage door of the Charter Theatre. He was shaking all over and waiting for the police to arrive, a cup of tea next to him ready to be drunk. He didn't subscribe to the theory that a cup of tea solved all the world's problems, and really could've done with a whisky or two instead. But that's what the security guard had placed in front of him before disappearing on his rounds.

Jason couldn't stop thinking about Jesse Morgan, wondering if he'd been hurt in the shoot-out. For all he knew he might be bleeding to death while he was sitting here looking at a cup of tea. But what else could he have done but run? The stalker was after him, so if he'd hung around he would've been shot as well. And what about that awful Vivian woman? He was pretty sure she'd been shot too. He had heard her screaming.

Then he started thinking about his two guitars that he'd left at the scene, about three thousand pounds' worth altogether. They were both insured, but he would hate to lose them. His sports bag was there as well. Hopefully someone from the hotel would put them aside until the police arrived.

Then he started feeling guilty that he was worrying more about his guitars than about Morgan. Jesus! What a mess. He stood up and paced around, looking warily out of the windows in case the stalker had followed him.

Calista Shaw and Hoss had just been leaving when he'd staggered in through the stage door, wet and out of breath.

They had looked at him as if he were mad, and had disappeared before he'd had time to explain anything. That was just as well with him. He doubted they'd believe it anyway. They would be travelling to Ireland for four days, while Jason could go back to Woodvale. They would meet up again for the London concert, but Jason wondered if he'd be fit to play another concert if this madman was still on the loose.

He sat back down at the desk and watched the security TVs. He saw figures popping in and out of view. He wished he'd got a glance of the stalker, so at least he'd know what he looked like for future reference, but all he'd seen was Morgan's back contorting with bullets before he'd turned and run. He was sure that was the only thing he could've done. What other alternatives were there? He was a singer for Chrissakes, not a policeman or a hero. He would make sure the police knew that when they eventually turned up to question him.

He was in the police station all night, being transferred back and forth from a cell to an interview room. They gave him a good grilling at first, and it reminded him a little of the grilling Jesse Morgan had given him after the Gator case had ended. Morgan hadn't believed him then, and the two policemen questioning him tonight weren't too impressed either. He told them the whole story, about the brick through his window and Julie Beech's broken nose, and Morgan being along as a bodyguard, but it was too bizarre for them to comprehend. He told them to ring Woodvale police station and check to see if Julie Beech existed, and after they'd done that they started giving him a little leeway. But he still had to stay there all night, catching a little sleep in between being questioned.

He tried finding out about Morgan, but they were reluctant to tell him. They told him Vivian had died before the ambulances arrived, but he didn't find out about Morgan until seven in the morning, when they finally came to tell him he could go.

Then they told him that Jesse had been shot three times and was in intensive care.

They gave him a lift to the station; it was a grey and windy day and not very inspiring.

Jason had his two guitars and sports bag back, which had been dusted for prints and were still covered in white. He couldn't carry everything now that Morgan wasn't around to help him, so he had to use a luggage cart. He thought about Morgan's suitcase that was sitting in a hotel somewhere. He hadn't known the name of the place, so the police were ringing round to retrieve it.

Jason found a seat on the first train heading south, away from everyone else, and put the two guitars in the rack above his head. He left the sports bag in the racks by the automatic doors, half hoping someone would pinch it so he wouldn't have to carry the damn thing. Then he slumped down in his seat, put his personal stereo on and listened to Bruce Springsteen's *Nebraska* album, which was about as bleak as he felt.

He had bought a quarter-bottle of whisky at the station, and he sipped it slowly and tried to lose himself, but he couldn't lose the guilty feeling about Morgan, even though the police in Preston had told him that running had been the best thing to do. They said Morgan should've phoned for back-up, shouldn't have tried to do it on his own. That had made Jason feel better at the time, but those guilty feelings were coming back by the truckload now. He felt the tears come into his eyes and he let them fall down his cheeks. He looked at the passing countryside and silently wept for Morgan. He didn't care if anyone saw him.

A little later when the refreshments man came along with his trolley, Jason had to buy some ginger ale and get a plastic cup because the taste of neat whisky was too much for him.

By the time the train pulled into London three hours later, the bottle was all gone and he was feeling quite drunk. He staggered off with his things and looked for a luggage cart.

He pushed his load to the Underground sign, but couldn't face the thought of going into the tube system. Instead he went to the taxi rank and lined up in a very long queue. It took him thirty minutes to get a ride, and he told the driver to take him to Victoria station.

His bladder was at bursting point by the time he reached Victoria, so he got a young woman on the station to mind his guitars while he went downstairs to the toilet. By some awful coincidence the piped music was playing Rod Stewart singing 'The First Cut Is The Deepest', Jason's first cover version of the tour which Morgan had said he'd liked, and that just started him off again. The tears fell almost as quickly as the piss coming out of him, and he was getting a few strange looks. He pulled himself together but had to wash his face before going back upstairs. No one stopped to ask if he was OK.

He felt so sleepy on the ride down to Redgate that he had to ask the man opposite to wake him if he nodded off. He did drift away, and the man politely gave him a nudge at the appropriate time. Then it was another struggle with his belongings, and far too many steps to encounter on his way down to the taxi rank. He told the driver his address in Woodvale, and perked up at the familiar surroundings. He was glad to be going back home.

The first thing Teddy Peppers did after driving away from Preston was to look for the appropriate cash machine for Vivian's cards. He found one quite quickly in the next town along, parked in the street and marched up to the machine. Once he'd put in the card and her pin number the machine told him that the most he could withdraw was three hundred pounds. That was ample for now, and when he asked for a balance he saw that she had over four thousand pounds! He wished he could withdraw the whole lot, but a bit each day would have to do. Then he looked at his watch. It was nearly midnight. In a few hours he could collect some more, and maybe get away with one more withdrawal the day after that. Then he would have to throw the cards away.

He drove on, not knowing which direction to go, then found himself on the M6 heading south. According to the tour schedule, Campbell would now be heading to Northern Ireland for four days, but there was no way Teddy was going over there, so he supposed he would just lie low in London and pick the tour up again on Sunday. He could hit a few nightspots and try and pick up some younger women. So he kept on driving and following the London signs.

He thought of Vivian as he drove, and was pretty sure she was dead. He had shot her several times in the chest and she'd screamed her head off when she went down. Silly bitch. The first shots had hit the bearded man and then he'd thought Vivian might as well go too, as she was definitely the type to blab. He'd been getting bored with her anyway. He'd fucked her in every position he knew so what further use was she? He'd find a younger woman in London, or maybe he'd just work alone from now on. He was usually better on his own. No one else to fuck things up.

A few miles further down the road he figured out that he'd seen the bearded man with Campbell at the theatre. He had been standing next to Campbell when Vivian went to talk to them. He was probably his manager or a roadie or something. No one of great importance. And then he remembered that as he was leaving the hotel room he had seen a guitar and sports bag sitting on the floor a few yards away. So Campbell had obviously been there, hiding behind the bearded man, before running away. So that was cool too. Now Campbell had seen him in action, and knew that he meant business. And that would put the fear of God in him. Things hadn't turned out too badly after all.

Teddy yawned but kept on driving.

19

Detective Sergeant Ian Kiddie heard the news about his friend when he went to work on Wednesday morning on the six o'clock shift. PC Rooney was standing at the front desk when he arrived and that was the news she hit him with. Morgan had been shot three times: in the side of the head, the lower abdomen, and his thigh, and was in intensive care. Kiddie stood there in shock for a while, not knowing what to do. He pried Rooney for more details but that was all she knew at the moment.

Kiddie walked out of the station to get some air, and found himself heading down the hill towards Naughton Road. When he got there he rang the doorbell of number eight and Officer Hoad, who had just started his morning shift, answered it. Kiddie told him the bad news over a cup of tea and asked him to get Jason Campbell to give him a ring as soon as he returned. Then he walked back up the hill to the station, where he sat in the canteen waiting for Superintendent Cole to turn up. His official starting time was nine o'clock but he usually got there a bit earlier. Kiddie then took another cup of coffee and sat at Morgan's desk, wondering if he'd ever see his friend again.

Half an hour later there was a commotion in the corridor. Kiddie poked his head out to see that Cole had arrived and was fending off questions by other officers. He pointed at Kiddie as he walked past and motioned for him to follow. They went into Cole's office and shut the door behind them.

'Any news on Jesse?' Kiddie asked.

'Not much more than you know,' Cole said. He looked a

little sleepy and harassed. 'Shot three times, lost a lot of blood. He was in a critical condition, then a stable condition, but now he's drifted into a coma. They don't understand why that's happened.'

'Shit,' Kiddie said, slumping into a chair.

'I'm sorry,' Cole said, and sat behind his desk.

'Any news on the shooter?'

'Not much,' Cole said, taking out a notebook from an inside pocket. 'A man in his mid-thirties with short dark hair who was staying at the hotel with a woman called Vivian Jones. They had been there two nights. According to Jason Campbell, Vivian Jones came to the concert he was performing at, and offered to put him up for the night. Apparently, and I find this hard to fathom, Campbell was asking from the stage for somewhere to stay the night to save money. His expenses for the tour come out of his performance fee of £100 per night.'

'Could be risky. Shouldn't be though in normal circum-stances.'

'Unless you're being followed by a stalker.'

'Agreed. And Morgan went along with this?'

'Apparently. They did it in Aberdeen and South Shields. Preston was the third time.'

'Third time unlucky.'

Cole nodded. 'Maybe Morgan saw it as a way of enticing the stalker. A dicey game to play though.'

'So this Vivian Jones invites them back and the stalker's waiting for them at the hotel?'

'Yes. Campbell said Morgan suspected something was up, but didn't want to phone for back-up in case he was wrong.'

'Bad move.'

'He told Campbell to stay back as Mrs Jones opened the door to the room. Then the shooting started.'

'And Vivian Jones was killed?'

'Yes. We're trying to track down relatives but her handbag

was nowhere to be found. And her name being Jones doesn't make it any easier.'

'Did she leave a credit card number at reception?'

'No. They were going to pay when they checked out.'

'So what happens now?'

Cole looked up from his notes and pushed his chair back. He must've been telephoned at home for him to know so much, Kiddie thought. And hadn't had much sleep since.

'We're getting full co-operation from the Lancashire police but we don't really know who we're looking for. So our best bet now is to keep this Campbell fellow on tour, but put an armed officer with him this time. I want someone with a gun to travel with him. Someone who's authorized, of course, and has a good record with weapons. Who do we have?'

Kiddie had to think about that one. Only certain officers at police stations were authorized to use weapons. They had to go through rigorous psychological and physical training and were reassessed annually. Had anyone ever used a firearm at Woodvale? Not in recent years, Kiddie thought. But then a light went on in his head and he remembered a conversation he'd had with Morgan once in the Red Lion, and he had to smile at the logicality of it.

'I can only think of one person,' he said, 'and from what I was told she's a shit-hot shot.'

Cole looked surprised. 'A she?'

'Julie Beech sir,' Kiddie said. 'Quite a good choice don't you think?'

Kiddie watched it sink in and a rare smile came over Cole's face. 'I would call that poetic justice,' he said.

There was a woodlouse walking around on Jason's ceiling and he lay in bed watching it. He had seen woodlice on his kitchen floor many times but how the hell did one get upstairs and into his bedroom and then on to the ceiling? He hated the things. He imagined it dropping off while he was asleep and into his mouth. That thought was enough to get him up. He clambered on to the bed with a magazine and swiped the thing away. He didn't see where it landed but at least it was at ground level now. He grabbed his dressing gown and went downstairs.

He could hear voices in the living room, so he went in and found Officer Hoad and another policeman. This one was tall with red hair and a moustache. He introduced himself as Detective Sergeant Ian Kiddie.

'How are you feeling now?' he asked Jason.

'A bit of a headache,' Jason said. 'But that was because I got drunk on the way home. Any news on Jesse?'

'Not good, I'm afraid. But Jesse's a tough nut. I have every faith in him.'

'I hope so, because I don't know how I'll be able to live with this. I should have dropped out of the tour from the start, and just waited for the stalker to turn up here. Then this never would have happened.'

Kiddie looked at Hoad. 'Let's all sit down for a moment.'

They sat down and Jason listened to a five-minute lecture about how it wasn't all his fault. He could hear this a hundred times, though, and it wouldn't change the way he felt. He glanced at the clock on the video machine and it said four o'clock. He'd been asleep all day. Now he wouldn't be able to sleep at night. He'd have to have a few drinks again to knock himself out.

'Now the conclusion we've come to,' Kiddie was saying, 'is that we'd like you to carry on with your tour, and this time we'll send an armed officer with you, a crack shot in fact. We see this as the quickest way of flushing the stalker out.'

Jason was all ears again. 'You've got to be joking. How can I tour after all this?'

'It's what Jesse would want. He'd want us to catch this madman, and you're our best chance.'

'Maybe the bastard will lie low for a while. Especially when he finds out he's shot a policeman.'

'He won't know he's shot a policeman. We're keeping it from the press. As far as they're concerned, he was your manager. And that's the story we'd like you to stick to.'

It was all like a sick joke, Jason thought. A game of cops and robbers. All stemming back to taking the wrong lodger into his house two years ago. What a major mistake that had turned out to be.

'Do I have any choice in the matter?' he asked.

'You always have a choice,' Kiddie said. 'It's a free country. The armed officer we have in mind is Julie Beech. You know her, of course.'

'Julie Beech? She's a firearms officer?'

'One of the best, apparently.'

'Hasn't she suffered enough already?'

'She's up for it. We've already asked her. She still doesn't look too great, but we've four days until you go back on tour. She'll be fine by then. And she's itching to get back at the man who broke her nose.'

From a purely selfish point of view Jason thought he would love to go on tour with Julie Beech. She was so good-looking, and they'd got on really well last time they'd been together. But on the trip home he had persuaded himself that the tour was over, the whole thing ruined. Was he really mentally fit enough to perform again?

'Can I think about it for a few hours?' he asked. 'I've only just got up and you've hit me with all this. I need a shower to clear my head.'

'No worries,' Kiddie said. 'Officer Hoad will be here all day.'

'Don't I know it,' Hoad moaned.

'So just tell him your decision. We'd like it to be a yes, though, or this could drag on for months. It'll be best to get it over and done with. And Julie Beech will be coming round to see you. Have a chat with her. Maybe that'll convince you.'

'When's she coming?'

'This evening. Sevenish.'

'Well, let me have a talk with her and then I'll let you

know,' Jason said. But he was already feeling a whole lot better knowing he'd be seeing Julie in a few hours' time.

He showered and shaved, put on some clean jeans and a denim shirt. His two lodgers, Dave and Geoff, were in for the evening, so when Julie arrived at seven, Jason suggested they go to a pub. She was wearing dark glasses to cover her two black eyes and was reluctant at first to go to a public place, but Jason convinced her. He tried not to stare at her broken nose.

They walked up the road to The Ringing Bell, which was never too busy on a Wednesday evening. They got a few odd looks when they entered, Jason feeling guilty that maybe people thought he was a wife-beater or something. He hadn't thought of that angle before. They took their drinks and sat in a quiet corner away from prying eyes.

'So, I hear you're a crack shot,' Jason said. 'A regular Annie Oakley.'

Julie smiled. 'No one at Woodvale has ever seen me shoot, so I don't know where they got that from. I do shoot regularly, though. I have to keep up to scratch.' Her voice was slightly different, as if she had a cold.

'So when did you learn?'

'When I was in the Met. I was twenty years old, and I thought it would be a challenge. I went through all the tests, passed the exams. It seems I have a natural talent for it. I have excellent eyesight, and a steady hand.'

'That's exactly what I need.'

'There are only about forty-five women in the Met who are allowed to shoot, against two thousand or so men. With a few others dotted around the country.'

'So you're part of an elite. I feel privileged. Cheers.'

He held up his wineglass and chinked it against hers. Julie was drinking white, Jason red.

'And what kind of gun do you use? Not that I know anything about guns.'

'It's a Smith and Wesson .38-calibre revolver. Six shots. Best used under a distance of twenty-five yards. Will that be enough?' she teased.

'Should be. I can't imagine any long-distance shooting being needed.'

'Actually, it can be used up to a distance of fifty yards. If you're a good shot. I practise at that distance at the range.'

Jason sipped his wine. 'The only problem might be the gun the stalker's carrying. If he shot Jesse three times and the Jones woman four times, he must be carrying an automatic, mustn't he?'

'That's good. Now you're starting to think like a policeman,' Julie said.

'I hope not.'

'It's best if you start thinking that way. Two heads are better than one. Anyway, if he took seven shots to knock two people down I would say he's a bad shot and doesn't know what he's doing. But I'll bear that in mind. There's a Glock I can take out instead, which has seventeen rounds. Would you feel happier with that?'

'I'll leave it up to you,' Jason said, finding it impossible to believe that he was sitting in a pub with a policewoman talking about guns. If his mother could see him now. Which reminded him that he'd better give his parents a ring and let them know what was going on.

'One thing you won't be doing this time round,' Julie said, 'is asking for places to stay from the stage. We stay in hotels all the way.'

'Fine with me,' Jason said. 'That method has lost its appeal with me, too.'

'And we're going by car. I'll be driving in an unmarked police car, all expenses paid. So bring what you like this time. No need to hold back on the luggage.'

'That'll be great,' Jason said. 'I'm looking forward to it already.'

They stayed in the pub for another half-hour, and then

walked back to Naughton Road. Julie got into her car and Jason waved goodbye. He couldn't wait for the tour to begin again, now. He felt as if he could fall for this unusual twenty-five-year-old, but would she be interested in someone over forty? He would find out some of the answers on the road.

Back in the basement, Jason started strumming his guitar, wondering whether to write a song about Julie. Then he started wondering if any songs had already been written about 'Julies'. The only one he could think of was an old pop song from the early seventies called 'Julie Do Ya Love Me'. He couldn't remember who it was by, but could remember the corny chorus. He strummed through it a few times but felt stupid singing it.

Then he thought of the old pop song 'Judy In Disguise', which had been a big hit when he was at school in the late sixties. It was sung by John Fred and the Playboy Band, their only UK hit. Jason started strumming through it, surprising himself with how many of the words he could still remember. He changed the title to 'Julie In Disguise', and it fit the song perfectly. Especially the bit about 'with glasses'; Julie had been wearing sunglasses to hide her black eyes. What could be more appropriate?

He left the basement and went upstairs to his bedroom and his CD collection, wondering if he had the song somewhere on a compilation. He would like to learn all the words and then sing it to her sometime. He hummed it over and over while he looked. He was getting hooked on it all over again.

20

With a four-day break until the London concert was due, Teddy Peppers found a cheap hotel in Earl's Court, and as soon as he checked in, bleached his hair white. He examined himself in the mirror afterwards, and liked his new look very much; he thought he looked like the racing driver Jacques Villeneuve.

He left Vivian's Polo in a small car park at the back of the hotel and caught the tube everywhere, although he found the crowds disturbing. In prison, everyone is very polite and gives you your own space; if they bump into you, they apologize straight away, to help keep the peace. Not so on the outside. He found most people extremely rude and grumpy. He'd like to see them survive seven years inside.

After rifling through Vivian's handbag, Teddy had been delighted to discover that some of her credit cards only had V. Jones stamped on them, so after perfecting her ordinary signature he was able to go out and use them for meals. He was also drawing out the three hundred pound cash limit every day from her Visa card, and would continue until the machine ate it up.

Teddy felt things were going his way now, and that shooting Vivian and the bearded man had been a positive turning point in his adventure. He had learned from the newspapers that Vivian had died – no great loss – and that the beardy was in fact Campbell's manager, although no name had been given out because he was on the critical list and they were having problems contacting his family. So now all Teddy had to do was to kill Campbell and then disappear into Europe for a while, where he could hang out in some bars and spend a bit of Vivian's money.

As he lay in his hotel room, Teddy found himself thinking a lot about Phil Gator, and wished he was around to talk to. Gator would've been excited by the hotel shoot-out and escape, and would no doubt be encouraging him to shoot more people were he around. Well, Teddy would call it a day after Campbell, making it three in total, a tally to be proud of, but still some distance behind Gator's.

Thinking about his old friend made Teddy feel horny. He masturbated three times during the day, and on Thursday decided it was time to go out and get some real flesh. Vivian had been all right for starters, but now it was time to get a younger woman.

So in the evening, wearing black leather trousers and a red shirt under his black leather jacket, he caught a tube on the District Line to the Embankment and walked into the West End. He found a club called the Hippodrome on Leicester Square and queued up with a bunch of youngsters to get in. He was almost slobbering at the mouth, seeing so much young flesh around, and he wondered if maybe he was too old for such a crowd. But after a few drinks to give him confidence, he homed in on a tarty blonde called Stacey, who was wearing a black miniskirt with a white halter top. She told him she was twenty-two and he had his tongue down her throat in under an hour. She invited him back to her flat in New Cross and they fucked into the early hours before falling into a drunken sleep. After showering together in the morning, Teddy made his way back to his hotel in Earl's Court.

He rested during Friday and then went out again in the evening, this time hitting a table-dancing club called Sensual near Hammersmith that a bouncer at the Hippodrome had told him about. Places like this hadn't existed when he'd last been a free man, and he spent over a hundred pounds in a couple of hours. There was a long, low stage on which a succession of women danced, stripping down to bare breasts and G-strings, while other girls moved through the audience. The audience girls would sit and talk with him awhile, and then ask if they could do a dance for him. It cost him ten pounds a time for a three-minute private dance, during which they would strip off their top and wiggle their G-stringed arse under his nose. After the first few times Teddy didn't find the experience particularly erotic, like maybe they were taking the piss out of him, but found he couldn't say no whenever a new girl came over; he just had to see them naked in front of him. As his wad of money quickly dwindled, though, he decided it was time to leave. He reckoned he'd had seven private dances in all, seven naked women within touching distance; not bad for a man just out of jail.

He decided to catch a tube back to the West End, where he caught a few drinks in two packed pubs before they closed. He felt like an outsider among all the laughing youngsters. He felt some destructive jealous feelings surfacing. He stumbled out into the night and it reminded him of the science-fiction film *Blade Runner*; oddly dressed people, bright lights and hardly any room to move, late-night restaurants and food stalls, broken bottles and litter on the ground, traffic at a standstill. He fought his way into the Underground and it was just as bad down there: drunken people singing, beggars, torn newspapers everywhere and mice running wild all over the tracks. He thought that maybe tomorrow he would have a quiet night in.

On Saturday, after showering and shaving, he caught a tube to the Embankment again and walked over the Thames to the South Bank Centre to check out where the Queen Elizabeth Hall was. He found it, no problem, and walked around the large modern complex looking for potential exits and getaways. The stage door was in a promising location, set back a bit off a quiet slip road. The hall itself was locked up for now, so he went to the Festival Hall and bought a ticket for the show at the box office. He nearly fainted at the price of sixteen pounds. It had only been a tenner in Preston.

He wandered around awhile, bought a beer in one of the bars and took it outside to a table by the river's edge. He looked at passing boats and at the trendy intellectuals sitting around him. He felt superior to them all. He felt that planning to kill someone took more intellect than reading a book or seeing a film. He wished he had a machine gun so he could mow them all down.

Julie Beech spent the four-day break resting and hoping her black eyes would heal by Sunday. They seemed to improve a little day by day, but it wasn't fast enough for her. As for her broken nose, she was trying to deal with it in a realistic way, but knew it would take a long time to come to terms with. She was having trouble breathing through her left nostril, but the doctor said that would improve with time. She found herself bursting into tears several times a day whenever she saw herself in a mirror, and she couldn't wait to come face to face with the bastard responsible. She remembered his face vaguely from the split second she'd seen him at the basement door. She reckoned he was only about five-nine, medium build, and wasn't the scariest-looking criminal she'd ever seen. Most criminals tended to look fairly normal, and it wasn't until you saw their rap sheet that you discovered how bad they were. But she wouldn't be asking too many questions when she found him. If he so much as blinked she would fill him full of lead, and being an authorized shot, she was entitled to do so in the right situation.

On Thursday she caught a train into London to visit her gun club, which was hidden under a converted railway arch near London Bridge station. It was run by two ex-army brothers called Ben and Olly Payne, and Julie had been a member for over three years. She liked practising here rather than at the police range; apart from the Paynes, no one knew she was a policewoman.

It was a small place used mainly by frustrated city types who wanted to let off steam on something a little more sophisticated than a football field. At reception there were league tables pinned up showing weekly marksmanship averages, and a large cabinet holding trophies that the Paynes had won over the years. There was a small upstairs bar to the left, and on the right the underground shooting gallery.

After firing off a hundred rounds, Julie went to the bar for an orange juice. Ben Payne asked about her nose and sympathized with her. Then a couple of guys in suits started talking, trying to chat her up. Julie answered their questions politely but wasn't fooled by their flirting routine, although she supposed it was a compliment to be chatted up in her present state.

She had never met a man she fancied at the club, and the thought of going out with a shooter didn't appeal to her at all. She knew how obsessed men could get with their weapons, and conversations about guns didn't interest her that much. She just enjoyed the sport because she was very good at it, and that was about as far as it went. She finished her drink and caught the train back to Redgate.

She thought about Jason Campbell on the journey, and found herself looking forward to seeing him again. Although he was a lot older than she was, they seemed to get on quite well, maybe because their worlds were so different. She thought it would be fun to go on a music tour and see behind the scenes, and her overtime would increase too. She'd be putting in long, not very strenuous hours.

At Redgate she jumped into a taxi to take her back to her flat in Woodvale. Trains did go to Woodvale, but the connections were infrequent, so taxis were the better bet. Except today she had an arsehole for a driver who looked at her in the rear-view mirror and said, 'Had a rough time last night, love?'

Julie took her ID out of her jacket and flashed it at him. 'If you open your mouth again I'll book you,' she said.

She looked out of the window, surprised by her little outburst. She supposed there was a lot of pent-up aggression waiting for release. She hoped the next time it came out the stalker would be standing in the way.

21

The soundcheck for the Queen Elizabeth Hall was at five o'clock on Sunday afternoon. Jason was picked up at his house by Julie Beech at three-thirty, and she helped him load up the car. She was wearing sunglasses again, and Jason couldn't get 'Julie In Disguise With Glasses' out of his head now; he kept singing it over and over. Later on in the car she took them off briefly and Jason said, 'Your eyes look a lot better.'

Julie smiled and said, 'You should see how much make-up I've got on.'

They drove up through Purley and Croydon, a slightly different route to the one Jason always took. When one of Julie's Dylan tapes had finished playing, Jason slipped one of his own into the tape machine. 'You should hear this,' he said. 'Much more tuneful.'

They listened in silence to the first track, 'Brave Girl', which was about a young woman fighting cancer. Jason thought it was a good song and not quite as depressing as it sounded. He had recorded the tape a few years ago in a studio in East Grinstead, where he'd laid down twelve of his songs in a day. Then he'd sent the DAT off to be duplicated and imaginatively called it 'Twelve Songs'. He'd since sold over two hundred copies of the cassette around the clubs, so he was making a small profit on it now.

When the song had finished Julie said, 'That was nice. Is it a true story?'

'Yeah,' Jason said. 'An old friend of mine. She went through hell, but always kept smiling. A lesson to us all.'

'How much do you sell those for?' Julie asked.

'Five pounds,' Jason said.

'Consider another one sold. There's a purse in my jacket pocket back there.'

'You can have it for nothing.'

'Thanks. Did Jesse Morgan buy one?'

'He never even heard it. I didn't take any on the road with me. Any more news on him?'

'No. He's still in a coma. They don't know when he's going to wake up. It's all a bit worrying. Ian Kiddie said he was going up to visit him.'

When they arrived at the South Bank Centre, Julie parked next to the artists' entrance of the Queen Elizabeth Hall. They were by the entrance to the National Film Theatre as well, so there were quite a few people wandering around.

'This is too busy for a shooter,' Julie said, lifting a guitar from the boot. 'It'll be worse when we leave. It'll be dark and quiet by then.'

'And that's a great place for someone to hide,' Jason said, pointing behind Julie to an area where skateboarders hung out. It was a cavelike place, formed where the Queen Elizabeth Hall was built on cement stilts. There were plenty of them to hide behind and the area was already slightly dark, even in daylight. There were ramps and different levels for the skateboarders to ride on, and members of the public usually just walked around it. You felt as if you were trespassing if you walked through.

Julie looked at it and said, 'That's not what I wanted to see. I don't like the look of that at all.'

'Me neither,' Jason said. 'I hope you've got your gun on.'

Julie pulled back her coat to reveal a holster around her waist.

They took the rest of the gear inside and signed in at the door with the security guard.

Julie flashed her ID at him and said, 'If anyone asks to see

Jason, we don't want to see them. But I'd appreciate it if you could get a good description.'

'No visitors at all,' the security guard nodded.

'Thanks,' Julie said, and then they followed Neil from PMA who had appeared from nowhere, who took them to the dressing rooms.

Teddy Peppers had already picked the skateboarders' haven as his place of attack, but he was sitting on a step just inside the entrance to the Museum of the Moving Image when he saw Campbell and a woman arrive. He wondered who she was.

He left his position and went to see if there was a film he could watch, as he still had two and a half hours to wait until the concert began. He had a choice of two from the cinemas in the complex, and he picked one called *Palookaville*. He had never heard of it but he liked the title, and it wasn't too long.

As the film unfolded, something was nagging at the back of his mind; the woman who'd been outside with Campbell, hadn't he seen her before somewhere? He thought about it for most of the film, and then got it towards the end. She was the policewoman he had punched in Campbell's house, but now she looked different because she had a broken nose. Teddy found that part quite amusing, but he also took it as an insult that they were now sending just a policewoman to protect Campbell. Did they think Teddy was such a small threat that he didn't warrant someone tougher? Especially after he had just shot two people?

So that settled it. Tonight he would show them.

There would be two more people he would be filling with lead.

And then it would be too late for them to take him seriously.

Julie stayed with Jason all the time leading up to the concert.

She watched from the side of the stage as he did his soundcheck, walked back with him to the dressing room afterwards and then went with him into the artists' bar for a drink and a snack.

Jason sat with a glass of wine and a sandwich he'd brought with him. Julie had a glass of mineral water and a packet of crisps. There were two TVs high on the wall, one showing the stage they had just vacated, the other showing another stage. Julie asked Jason where it was.

'That's the Purcell Room,' he said. 'A much smaller venue. Used mainly for classical recitals. It's in the same building.'

'There are TVs everywhere,' she said. They had already seen one just outside the dressing rooms in a lounge area. You could watch the whole concert sitting on a sofa.

'It's the TV era,' Jason said. 'Every bar you go into these days has one. Five or six years ago there were hardly any of them.'

'That's because all you boys want to watch the football.'

'Yeah. It saves us having to talk to each other. I hardly go to pubs these days.'

'You were there the other night.'

'Those were special circumstances. Usually I just go to the off-licence.'

'Drinking at home alone?'

'Much healthier. No smoke and no yobs.'

'But no company either.'

'I don't need it most of the time.'

Julie took a sip of mineral water. She didn't drink much at all. Working shifts, she couldn't really afford to because it mucked up her body even more than the odd hours. She preferred staying sober.

'It could lead to problems,' she said.

Jason nodded. 'I started drinking a lot more after the Gator affair. I was a nervous wreck after that for over a year.'

'Didn't you ask for help? We could've put you in touch with someone.'

'I didn't want to see any more of the police. They were pretty tough on me at the time.'

'You could've gone to your doctor. He would've given you some pills or something. Recommended counselling.'

'I'd rather drink than pop Prozac. Anyway, it's not as if I drink all the time. Mainly evenings, really. Can we talk about something else?'

'What do you want to talk about?'

'How about, why are you so good-looking?'

'I'm not good-looking any more.'

'You're the best-looking woman I've seen for a long time. Broken nose or not.'

Julie had to smile. Was Jason being serious, or just a smoothie like most men? 'You'd better have another drink before you get out of control,' she said.

Teddy walked through the skateboarders' haven a few more times in the dark, looking at angles from which to shoot at Campbell's car. He could get pretty close to it, maybe twenty yards, then he would just have to let loose with a hail of bullets. Or maybe walk up to them and let them have it. Then he would run off into the maze of buildings and walkways, head back to the Underground and disappear.

There were six or seven skateboarders whizzing around, street urchins with nothing better to do. There were a few homeless people hanging around as well. If Teddy had his way he would chuck them all in the River Thames and just let them float away. He was wearing a dark blue ski jacket today so he wouldn't be so conspicuous among them. The Beretta fitted easily into the big side pockets and he felt like flashing it around, scaring them out of the area. It would be a lot easier if they weren't there.

At seven-thirty he walked up to the hall itself and pushed his way through the heavy metal doors. There were crowds of people in the foyer already: middle-aged, well-to-do, more than a few ageing hippies. Teddy thought that all the hair on view would be enough to start a forest fire. He got a few looks from people surprised at his bleached crop. He thought he looked the coolest dude in the place. He would look even cooler waving a Beretta around his head, raising holy hell.

He went into the concert hall and was shown to his seat by an old guy in a uniform. He felt very uncomfortable amid such opulence; he felt he didn't belong in such surroundings. It was more like a classical music venue than a country music venue. Music for stuffed shirts. He imagined if Campbell was playing in an orchestra instead of solo how much harder that would be. He wouldn't know who to shoot because they'd all be dressed like penguins, sitting behind their big instruments all looking the same. A nightmare!

He settled in his seat and waited for the show to begin.

From a prestige point of view, the London show was the biggest of the tour. There would be plenty of press to see Calista Shaw, and more than a few record industry types too. Although Jason knew his songs were pretty good, he still couldn't imagine himself getting a record deal, but he could always live in hope. He would have to perform his best here. He could feel the adrenaline running through his veins.

He looked at his watch. He was due on stage at seven-forty-five, the earliest show so far. Being predominantly a classical music venue, they were still stuck in that particular time zone. Calista Shaw would be getting to bed early tonight, he thought. He still hadn't seen her today, though, or Hoss. He wondered how they'd got on in Ireland. He wondered if they knew about the madman who was intent on sharing the tour with them, the surprise third act that wouldn't go away. The longer they didn't, the better, Jason supposed, but if there was any more trouble they were bound to find out. Neil from PMA said he'd keep it from them for as long as possible.

Jason reached for the toilet paper and wiped himself, pulled up his jeans and washed. He often had the shits before going on stage. He pulled the flush and walked into the dressing room, and there was Julie Beech sitting reading a magazine. 'You're going to know me very well by the end of this tour,' he said.

'All part of the job,' Julie said. 'Would you mind closing the door?'

22

They stood in a small corridor by the stage manager's office, waiting for signals for the show to begin. Neil was there too, half listening to their conversation, also waiting for the signal.

'How are you feeling?' Julie asked.

'Nervous,' Jason said. 'But I'll try not to think about things.'

'The stalker won't try anything in the auditorium. Not unless he's completely loopy.'

'You don't think he's completely loopy?' Jason asked, and Julie didn't have an answer to that question.

'You know, the best shows are done when you don't care about them,' Neil said, an occasional bass player in a band.

'Someone else told me that too,' Jason said. 'I care about this one, though. You never know who might be watching.'

'The eternal optimism of the musician,' Neil said.

And then they got the signal.

'Have a good one,' Neil said. 'Go get that recording contract.'

Jason laughed, stepped up to the stage and walked into the spotlight. He said 'hello' into the microphone to make sure it was working, and then plugged the lead into his guitar. He strummed a few times to make sure it was in tune and then introduced himself.

Standing on stage under spotlights, the only visible people are those in the first couple of rows. Jason always avoided looking at them because if he saw someone looking grumpy or not clapping it could put him right off his performance.

But standing there now, he homed right in on someone in the second row because the man had startlingly white hair, like an albino. He kept looking at him as he strummed and sang his first song, and he wondered who he was, because he looked very odd.

Teddy noticed Campbell looking at him throughout the set, and almost wanted to take the Beretta out of his pocket and point it at him, see if he could make him forget his words. He had to hand it to the boy, he looked so relaxed on stage you would think he might fall over. He was joking with the audience, and seemed a lot more at ease than he had in Preston. Obviously gaining in confidence with each show. It was a shame it would be his last.

The set was shorter tonight, though. Teddy only counted five songs, and it almost took him by surprise.

The house lights came up, and he pushed his way through the crowd who were making their way to the bar. Idiots. He had far more important things to do than drink.

Julie watched Jason leaving the stage, giving a little wave to the audience, and they seemed to love him all right. She wondered if she could end up loving him as well. 'That was great,' she said, patting him on the back as he walked into the corridor again.

'Felt great,' Jason said. 'This is what it's all about. You're sure we have to leave right now?'

'I'd rather get away as soon as possible. It's too risky going to meet your fans.'

'I'm not bothered about that, I just fancy a few drinks. But let's pack up and go. You're the boss.'

'I thought that was Bruce Springsteen?'

Jason laughed. 'Very good. A music joke.'

She followed him into the dressing room and put the black guitar in its case while Jason dealt with the other one. Julie liked the black guitar best because it looked so flashy, but the brown one had sounded very nice. She had watched the show from the couch outside, on the TV. There had been no one else around except a large American who said hello, who she presumed to be Hoss.

'Now you remember the routine?' Julie said, when they were ready to go.

'You pack everything in the car while I wait in the lobby. You put the keys in the car and start the engine. You come back in and get me and we both walk to the car. I get in and drive while you keep a lookout.'

'Very good. You learn fast.'

'I'm on a learning curve.'

They carried everything through the corridors to the front door. Julie asked the security man if anyone had asked for Jason and he said no. She was pleased about that. She walked out to the car on her own with one of the guitars and opened the boot. On her way back she looked around, mainly towards the skateboarders' area. It was very dark in there now, and she didn't like the look of it at all.

When everything was in the boot of the car, the engine running and both the front doors open, Julie came back for Jason, still looking around her. Jason felt quite relaxed looking at Julie heading towards him, her coat open down the front, the holster around her waist clearly visible. She had a serious look on her face, though, and he wondered why a twenty-five-year-old would want to get mixed up in business such as this. But he was very grateful that she was with him, and was totally under her command. She opened the foyer door and said, 'Let's go.'

They walked quickly towards the car and had nearly reached it when Jason heard the first shots winging over their heads.

Julie shouted at him to run and he didn't need to be told twice. There were people screaming around them as he jumped in the car, shut the driver's door, put it into gear and drove away. That was something else Julie had told him to do. If there was any trouble, he was to drive away and leave her there.

The passenger door shut by itself as he drove down the road. He was heading towards the skateboarders' haven where a man with white hair was shooting his gun towards the artists' entrance. He didn't seem to want to fire at Jason, but was more intent on firing at Julie.

Jason swerved to the left and put his foot on the accelerator, but then saw there was a junction up ahead. He would either have to drive right through and risk a crash, or stop.

Taking cover behind one of the cement pillars underneath the Queen Elizabeth Hall, Julie was counting how many shots were coming at her before she made her move. They were coming thick and fast and all over the place, and had smashed a few windows behind her in the cinema complex. She hoped no one had been hurt.

Then there was a pause and she took this to be reloading time for the madman, and it was time to make her move. So she peeked out from behind the pillar and ran to the next one.

As she was doing so, she saw a car approaching from the left, headlights blazing, heading straight for where the gunman was. Then to her horror she realized it was the unmarked car, and that Jason was driving it! She watched it bump over the kerb into the skateboarders' area and then saw a man with white hair running away. She started running herself shouting at Jason to stop.

Jason was having the time of his life. The stalker was right in front of him in the headlights, and now they were heading down the walkway by the side of the Thames. He could see Julie sprinting after him in the mirror, and people were screaming and scrambling out of his way. He slowed the car down and let Julie catch up. He leaned over and opened the passenger door for her.

She jumped in screaming: 'Let's get the bastard!'

Teddy was running for his life, not believing that a car had come at him over the kerb. Who the hell was driving that? Another policeman?

He kept running towards some steps, so he could vanish up those and stop the car from following. Then he sensed the car slowing and then starting again. What the hell was going on? He waved the gun in the air to get people out of the way, and it had the desired effect.

Julie saw the man with the white hair vanish up some steps to another level and told Jason to pull over. She told him to stay in the car, and flew out of the door in pursuit.

She was a good runner, jogged at least three times a week, so if the madman wanted a long chase she was up for it. She felt a controlled rage inside her and really wanted to catch this man who had disfigured her for life. But when she reached the next level she knew it was a hopeless chase. There were so many turnings, and more staircases: he could be anywhere.

She stopped and thought about it, hoping she would hear a commotion somewhere, but everything was quiet. Common sense told her it was too risky to continue; she could be walking into an ambush. It would be safer just to let him go this time and catch him later. He was sure to be back. It was turning into a game. She put her gun back in its holster and tried to calm her breathing.

23

They would laugh about all this sometime later, Jason was sure, but for now it was all very serious, a very serious mess. He was in an interview room at the Charing Cross police station giving a statement to a uniformed policeman. He was getting used to these interview rooms. Maybe he'd redecorate his bedroom like one. There was something very Zen about them.

And then the officer left the room and Julie came in and sat down opposite.

'Are you going to rough me up?' he said. 'I don't mind.'

'I should do. Why on earth did you drive after him?'

They hadn't had a chance to talk since the incident. When Julie had got back to the car, the police were already there.

'I couldn't drive off and leave you,' Jason said. 'I left Jesse when the shooting started and look what happened to him. I was going down the road thinking, no, this isn't going to happen again. If you'd been shot, I wouldn't have been able to live with myself.'

'That's all very noble, but I wouldn't have been shot. I'm a trained officer.'

'So was Jesse.'

'Not in firearms. He was unprepared. I was about to jump him when you came crashing over the kerb.'

'You think you would have caught him?'

'I had a pretty good chance. He was out of bullets and I hadn't even fired once. I had seventeen warm ones for him.'

'I'm sorry. I just didn't want to feel such a coward this

time. I also felt a coward when you got punched on the nose. I couldn't do anything to help you then, either.'

'I'm glad you didn't. It's not your job.'

'Well, I'm glad I did it anyway.'

She smiled at him but then got serious again. 'Would you like the bad news first, or the good?'

'I'll take the bad news.'

'You're going to be charged with dangerous driving. You endangered other people's lives.'

'For fuck's sake! What was the shooter doing, for Chrissakes?'

'Well, he'll get charged when he's caught. But you know, they have to do this by the book. We're all very regimented.'

'More like demented.'

'They also want you to stop doing the tour. It's too dangerous to the public if this shooter keeps turning up all the time, spraying bullets everywhere. In fact, they're forbidding you to do the tour.'

'Great. I wish they'd make their minds up. I was ready to quit when Jesse got hurt.'

'I know. It's just that they've never had a situation like this before. They don't really know what they're doing.'

'Well, at least I got the London show in. That was the most important one.' In a way Jason felt relieved that it would be over, although he would have liked to spend some time with Julie. But it was too risky carrying on like this; it was all getting out of hand. The police were right. They couldn't go on like a travelling Wild West show.

'Do you have to ring anyone? Tell them you've dropped out?' Julie asked.

'Yeah, I'd better ring Neil.'

Julie took a mobile phone from her pocket and handed it to him. Then she stood up to leave.

'Julie?' Jason asked, getting his address book from an inside pocket, trying to appear casual. 'Will I see you again, or are you going to disappear from my life as well?'

When he looked up she had a cheeky grin on her face. 'I forgot to tell you the good news. I'm going to be looking after you at your house. I'll be your twenty-four-hour armed guard.'

'Great!' Jason said, and started punching in Neil's number.

It was all going a bit pear-shaped, as they always said on TV police programmes, and Teddy had seen enough of those inside. Things like Inspector Miserable Morse, and Inspector Fucking Frost. Programmes so unreal the public lapped them up. If they showed them the real world no one would watch them, they'd be too depressing. What annoyed Teddy most about them was that the criminal always got caught. OK, so he knew that ninety-one per cent of murders in Britain got solved, but why couldn't they have a few episodes where the bad guy got away? That would be a bit more fun at least. *Prime Suspect*, too. That was another one. Some of those had been OK at first, but it had got worse with each succeeding episode. He liked the actress though. She was pear-shaped as well. Teddy wouldn't mind a few nights with her. Get her to sit on his prime meat suspect.

He was lying on his bed at the cheap hotel in Earl's Court. It was in the early hours of Monday morning, and he couldn't sleep. He'd showered on returning to his room, getting rid of all the sweat from his run along the Embankment and then over to Waterloo station. It had been quite easy getting rid of the policewoman; there were so many different hiding places around that South Bank Centre. But he hadn't expected to be chased by a car. It was like something out of a James Bond movie. Quite unreal. He would've liked to have been a passer-by watching it, instead of a participant. No doubt a few of those would come forward and give the police a fine description of him. He would have to move on tomorrow. But to where?

He reached down to the side of the bed and picked up the piece of paper torn from *Q* magazine. Tonight's show was in

Cardiff, Tuesday's in Portsmouth. He was fucked if he was travelling to Cardiff, so it would have to be Portsmouth. A nice trip to the south coast. Almost on home territory. He let the piece of paper drop to the floor and closed his eyes. He wondered how much the cops knew about him so far.

They drove back to Woodvale at just after six in the morning. Julie was at the wheel, joking that there was no way Jason would drive this car again. Jason asked if he'd also get done for driving without insurance.

'Did anyone get hit by the madman's bullets?' he asked.

'A homeless person got hit in the arm,' Julie said. 'And there were a few broken windows at the cinema.'

'Where was the homeless person?'

'Sitting next to one of the concrete stilts. Settling down for the night.'

'He must've got a fright. A shoot-out suddenly taking place in front of him.'

'At least he got a bed for the night.'

Jason chuckled. 'Has he been questioned yet? He might have had a good view of the shooter.'

'He's been questioned but he was too drunk. Thought he was dreaming it.'

'Great. When are we ever going to learn something about this bloke?'

'Well, we know he's now got white hair. And a few people along the river are going to give descriptions of him.'

'He had red hair when he punched you.'

'So we know he dyes his hair a lot. He probably won't be white any more, though.'

The white hair thing was bothering Jason. He remembered back to the concert. Hadn't there been someone in the audience with white hair? In the second row? He tried to remember a face.

'Someone at the concert had white hair,' he said. 'Sitting in the second row.'

'Who was that, an old man?'

'No, a young guy. I spotted him during the first song. I thought he looked a bit weird. I try not to look at the audience usually, but he seemed so striking. Like an albino.'

Julie looked at him. 'Let's get this straight. There was a young, white-haired guy sitting in the second row for the whole of your set, or just part of it?'

'He was there the whole time. I kept glancing at him. He was looking straight back at me.'

'Why didn't you tell me this before?'

'I only just made the connection.'

'Do you think you could describe him to an artist?'

'I'll give it a go.'

'Good. I'll get a list of names of everyone in the front two rows.'

'They'll only have a name if he paid by credit card, and I doubt if he did that. Unless it was stolen.'

'Anything's worth a try at this stage.'

Jason couldn't argue with that.

Detective Sergeant Ian Kiddie had driven up to Preston on Sunday morning to the Sharoe Green Hospital, and spent a couple of hours in the afternoon sitting next to his best friend Jesse Morgan. Jesse was in a private room in Margaret Ward, a lot of apparatus surrounding him, tubes going in and out of his arms and body. It pained Kiddie to see his usually fit friend lying there looking white and thin, wearing a white smock like a baby in a nappy.

Jesse was still in a coma and Kiddie had taken a portable CD player in to play some country music to him. He had read about people coming out of comas after being played music, or tapes of relations talking to them, or after visits by famous footballers. There weren't any famous footballers in Preston any more, though, so country music would have to do.

He had asked several officers at Woodvale if they had any

in their collections, and had arrived with six CDs by people he had never heard of. He played them one after the other, cringing at some of the lyrics, thinking that this kind of music would drive most people to their deaths. The nurses had found it hilarious, though, steel guitars and nasal voices greeting them on their rounds, along with a large red-headed Scotsman reading a magazine with cotton wool stuffed in his ears.

In the afternoon he had checked into The Byron Lodge Hotel, and talked with the manager and staff about the incident the previous Tuesday. He tried to get descriptions of the shooter, but he'd only been seen once when they checked in, by the assistant manageress, and she'd already talked to the police. Then he went to the police station and had a chat with the senior officers there. It was all rather fruitless but had to be done.

In the evening he went back to the hospital and listened to some more country music. He reflected that it would be a cruel end to Jesse's life if he were to die so close to retirement. Isn't that what always happened in clichéd police films? Kiddie was determined that Jesse wouldn't go out in such a way, so he went on playing the CDs and kept his earplugs in.

24

It was always good to analyse things, and Jason was sitting in his basement on Tuesday morning doing just that. He had a guitar on his lap but he wasn't playing it at all. He was sitting staring at the white wall opposite. He was thinking about his dreams.

When Jason had been having money problems just over two years ago, his dreams at night had always been about losing his house. In those dreams he would be homeless: checking into run-down boarding houses, sharing rooms with strangers, having to queue for the bathroom or sleep in damp-infested bedrooms. They were mini-nightmares, he supposed, a reminder of a way of living he didn't want to go back to, those years of his past when he had lived in rented rooms, right up until his mid-thirties.

Then, when he had started getting some decent lodgers into his house, and his finances had improved, all those dreams had vanished almost overnight. It had been a big relief, but they had then been replaced by recurrent travel dreams that always took place on trains or buses. He would be travelling somewhere either by himself or with other people, and he would always be late getting there, or missing a connection and having to wait for hours, or arriving in a place he didn't know feeling totally lost. He took those dreams to mean that he didn't know where he was going in life, and they had persisted to this very day. They weren't as annoying as the house dreams, but if there was some way he could completely erase dreaming from his sleep, Jason felt he would be a happier man.

Lately though, another type of dream had been entering his nights, and these were dreams he had often had as a child: dreams where someone was chasing him and he couldn't run fast enough to get away. His legs would feel heavy as if embedded in mud, or as if someone was holding him back by his shirt. Luckily the bogeyman had never caught him in these dreams, but maybe it was only a matter of time.

Jason knew he was having these dreams because of the stalker who had entered his life, and that they would only disappear when he'd been caught. So he was quite glad to be off the tour now, quite glad to be at home waiting for the next attack, waiting for it all to be over so he could carry on with his normal life again.

He had telephoned Charles Penn at his London office yesterday and had a long chat with him. Penn had agreed that he should drop out of the tour and had taken it all without fuss. They would find another singer to fill in some of the southern dates, and Penn said that if the stalker was caught soon then maybe Jason could join the end of the tour and finish it off. Jason didn't know if he wanted to do the rest of the tour, but felt obligated to Penn now and couldn't turn him down. He would finish the job he'd started, and almost felt like hanging a sign at the front of the house telling the stalker he was home, just to get it all over with. The nutter didn't particularly scare him any more. His brief chase after him on Sunday had fired his manhood, and if Julie was around all the time he felt very safe. Maybe he should be more worried than he was, but he could save all that for his dreams. His waking hours would be filled with optimism from now on.

That same morning Julie Beech moved into 8 Naughton Road to start her period of 'constant protection', as Chief Superintendent Cole called it. The two lodgers, Dave and Geoff, had been asked to move out temporarily, and had moved in with their girlfriends. Neither of them had been too pleased about the situation, but had moved out quickly enough when Julie told them the stalker had already killed one person and wounded two others. Jason told them he would deduct their days away from next month's rent, so they had packed enough for a week and disappeared.

Julie moved into the large front bedroom that belonged to Geoff, while the other two police officers, Hoad and Brazier, were kept on their twelve-hour shifts downstairs in the front room.

The next-door neighbours weren't informed of the permanent police presence, even though there were now guns on the premises. It was never wise to tell anyone about such an operation because tongues would wag, and soon the whole neighbourhood would know about it. Better just to lie low and expose the operation when it was over, and then they could talk about it as much as they wanted. Dave and Geoff had also been told to hold their tongues.

Yesterday, after they'd arrived back in Woodvale, Julie had taken Jason to the police station where he had sat with an officer trying to make an E-fit of the man with the white hair at the concert. It had taken over an hour, but Jason had been pleased with the result, although his stalker now looked a little like Sting, albeit Sting with a bigger nose. The picture had been given to the press and Julie was looking at it now in the *Daily Mail* as she sat in her new room. She hoped someone somewhere would recognize the man and flush him out.

As her room belonged to Geoff, the antiques dealer, there was plenty of furniture lying around, old wooden things cluttering the floor space. Julie pushed most of it against the walls, being careful not to scratch anything, so she could get in and out of the room quickly if she needed to. She cleared a space in front of the bay windows and picked the most comfortable chair to place there. She would spend most of her time on her backside, although not so close to the window that she could be seen from outside. Officer Hoad was directly underneath in the living room on his day shift.

Julie folded the newspaper and dropped it on the bed. It was just after eleven, and she would go downstairs in a minute for a cup of tea and some biscuits. Jason was down in the basement, although she couldn't hear any music being played. It was a shame his tour had been cancelled, but he had told her he could join it again if the stalker was caught quickly. She thought she might join him for a few of the dates, and she would deserve a break when all this was over. It would be good to get away from Woodvale for a while.

She looked at the view that would be hers for the immediate future: the small garden directly below, a raggedy front hedge, Naughton Road and then another hedge on the other side of the road, rising into some trees. She had already walked along there earlier, and thought it an ideal place to watch the house from. There was a footpath running behind the hedge, and passing people couldn't be seen from where she was sitting. If she were the stalker, she would come from that direction rather than the back garden, where he might be seen from other houses.

Julie yawned and felt the break in her nose. She was getting used to it more each day, and her breathing was getting easier, but she was still really looking forward to coming face to face once again with the man responsible.

Having recovered from the unwanted excitement of Sunday evening, and having decided not to travel to Cardiff for Monday's show, it was a fairly relaxed Teddy Peppers who caught the train down to Portsmouth on Tuesday morning. He decided to leave Vivian's Polo in an Earl's Court street with the keys in the ignition, hoping that some villain would steal it and wrap it round a tree. Just to be doubly sure, though, he had wiped every surface that he'd touched in case the coppers found it first.

Teddy settled into his seat as the train pulled out of

Waterloo and started reading the newspaper he had bought for the journey. He nearly jumped out of his seat, though, when he saw an E-fit picture of himself, but then relaxed when he studied it some more. It didn't really look like him at all, too good-looking really, like that poncey singer Sting. But the report said he had white hair, and he knew he would have to change it again tonight. It said he was wanted in connection with a shooting at the South Bank Centre on Sunday night, where a down-and-out waster had been shot in the arm. Teddy had to laugh at that. He didn't think he'd hit anyone.

When he arrived in Portsmouth he caught a taxi to the Wedgewood Rooms in a place called Fratton. He paid the driver and stood outside the small, scruffy club, which had posters all over the front advertising forthcoming concerts. He looked at some of the names but didn't recognize any of them. Calista Shaw was there, though, together with Jason Campbell next to her in smaller writing. He looked up and down the street and headed off looking for somewhere to stay.

A woman's voice said, 'How is he?'

Ian Kiddie looked up from his magazine and pulled his earplugs out.

'Pardon?' he asked.

Standing in front of him was Nicola, the barmaid from the Red Lion, Jesse's old girlfriend. He hadn't seen her come into the room. He reached over to the portable CD player and turned the music down.

'Why are you playing that stuff so loud?' she asked. 'Trying to wake him up?'

'It's the thing to do,' Kiddie said. 'Play some of their favourite music in the hope of getting through to them.'

'That's Garth Brooks, though,' Nicola said. 'Jesse hates Garth Brooks. If you play more of that he'll never pull through.'

She walked over to the machine and pressed the stop button. Then she gave Kiddie a stern look. 'You still haven't answered my question.'

Kiddie tried remembering what the question had been. Wasn't that when he'd said pardon? And why was Nicola in such a bad mood? She was normally very relaxed.

'The question being?' he asked.

'How is he?' she said, a bit too loudly.

'He's great, as you can see. Just taking a midday nap, and then he'll be up and about telling jokes. How the hell do you think he looks?' Kiddie could get stroppy himself when he wanted to.

'No need to get angry,' Nicola said, and went to sit by the bed.

Kiddie watched her take Jesse's hand and stroke it slowly. Then the tears started running down her cheeks and he sat there not knowing what to do. He decided to leave the room and come back later.

He walked past the nurse's desk and then took innumerable corridors and stairs before he arrived outside. He walked to the main entrance and bought a coffee at the Aroma shop, then sat at a table looking at all the sick people coming in and out. He had been in many hospitals over the years, and they always fascinated him. Different kinds of people, different kinds of illnesses. He didn't find them depressing at all, and the nurses were always friendly.

He wondered if he should stay in Preston any longer, whether it was really worth his while. It might take weeks or months for Jesse to snap out of his coma. And every day spent up here would be another day's holiday used up. Jesse would probably think he was mad. He would tell him to go back to work and stop worrying. Well, that was easier said than done.

He finished his coffee and made the long walk back to Margaret Ward. He pushed open Jesse's door and saw a red-eyed Nicola standing there with a CD in her hand.

'This is what you should be playing,' she said forcefully.

He felt like a school kid being told off. He looked at the CD and it said 'Calista Shaw' on it.

'Where did you get that?' he asked.

'It was in Jesse's coat pocket. A signed copy, too.'

He watched her walk to the CD machine and slot it in.

25

The inside of the Wedgewood Rooms reminded Teddy of some working-men's clubs he'd frequented in his youth: wallpaper stained with tobacco, tables running lengthwise from the stage and a gloomy, dark kind of atmosphere. The sort of place that might have a few strippers before the blue comedian comes on. More his kind of place, though, better than that stuffed-up Queen Elizabeth Hall. And the tickets were cheaper, too.

He was sitting in a chair at the back. There were several rows facing the tables, right next to the sound desk. He was sitting at the back because he was feeling a bit self-conscious. After checking into a pub for the night, he had found a barber and asked to have his head shaved. He didn't know why, it was an impulse thing, and now he wished he hadn't done it. It felt cold for one thing, and he looked like a real slaphead. He felt people looking at him, although it seemed to be quite fashionable these days. Lots of balding blokes did it rather than have just a bit of hair at the side. But after coming out of the barber's he had gone into a cold sweat when he realized that he now no longer had any hair to dye. What would happen if he were seen again? How would he change his appearance? He could no longer do his chameleon act. He was now a slaphead chameleon, and that was no use to anyone. He would have to wear a woolly hat or something, or maybe even a wig. Or maybe he should just get this whole folly over with and nail Campbell once and for all so he wouldn't have to keep changing any more. Then he could quietly slink away to Europe and take in some sun, the slaphead chameleon lying on a beach.

Slaphead chameleon.

The more Teddy said it to himself, the more he liked it. It had a kind of mythic ring to it.

He sipped his pint of lager and looked at his watch. He had scraped the face of it on one of those concrete stilts on Sunday. He could barely make out the numbers. He would have to buy another one, although money was getting low. Yesterday, Vivian's credit card had been eaten by the machine, so he had thrown all her others away as well. Something else to worry about. He would have to find another sucker to mug pretty soon.

Then the lights went down and a man walked on stage. He tapped the microphone twice and welcomed everyone to the Wedgewood Rooms. The place was almost full now.

'We have a slight change to our programme tonight,' the man said. 'Our original support act, Jason Campbell, has had to withdraw because of illness, so instead we have some local talent for you, a man you may have seen around the clubs in the past. Would you please give a big Portsmouth welcome to Pete Gibson!'

The crowd started clapping and whooping as a middle-aged man with a beard and guitar walked on stage. Teddy felt his anger rise as he left his seat. He stormed to the side door and walked out, and there was another bald man standing there with a few other people.

'What's happened to Jason Campbell?' Teddy asked. 'He's the bloke I came to see. I don't give a toss about the local talent.'

'Cancelled,' the bald guy said. 'He's ill.'

'Ill? I came all the way from London for this!'

'I'm sorry. I can't do anything about it. We were given short notice.'

Teddy felt desperate. All this way to Portsmouth for nothing. And a bald haircut as well. Just like the bloke talking to him. What a total fuck-up. He felt like he was talking to another egg.

'We can give you a refund,' the bald bloke said.

'Yeah, you do that,' Teddy said, and ran his hand over his scalp.

When he'd got his money he walked out of the door and wandered down the street in a bad mood. He felt like exploding on someone, picking a fight with the first person walking along. Not only was it a waste of time coming all this way, it was also a waste of money. He muttered swear words under his breath as he marched on.

He came to an off-licence and decided to buy some whisky for his hotel room. He could only afford a quarter-bottle, but that would be enough to do his head for several hours. There was a weaselly man behind the counter, wearing a name tag saying 'Ron, Manager'. He stank of booze as Teddy handed his money over.

'Been trying out the stock?' Teddy asked.

The man called Ron smiled at him. 'It's been a long day, but not too long to go now.'

'When do you shut?'

'Nine o'clock.'

'Well, have a good evening.'

Ron said thanks, and Teddy walked out and ambled towards what he thought would be the back of the shop, down an alley with a few quiet backyards. He looked at his watch. It was ten to nine.

In prison he had heard about an easy way to rob an off-licence, and he thought that now might be an ideal time to put it into action. After all, the only assistant looked half pissed already, and it would make his trip to Portsmouth less of a waste. How hard could it be?

So he walked the streets for another ten minutes, looking in rubbish bins for an empty paper bag, and then returned to the back door of the off-licence. The empty bag was a McDonald's one, and he poked two holes in it for his eyes and slid it over his head. It smelled a bit of chips, but it wasn't too unpleasant. And it slipped on nicely over his bald head.

It was now nearly five past nine. Teddy took the Beretta from his jacket pocket and rang the back doorbell. He could hear footsteps on the other side and then Ron was saying: 'Who is it?'

'I've got some glasses to return,' Teddy said. 'Am I too late?' He could almost hear Ron swearing under his breath, but a few seconds later the door swung open.

Teddy pushed himself in before the startled Ron could do anything. He shut the door behind him and pointed the gun at Ron's head. 'You shouldn't open the door after hours,' he said. 'Don't they teach you anything at management school?'

Ron had his hands in the air and was shaking like a leaf. He had spiky hair and was only about five-seven. A skinny runt, too. Teddy couldn't believe how easy this was going to be.

'They teach us to give you the money,' Ron said. 'Is that what you'd like?'

'You're a fast learner. Lead me to the safe.'

Teddy watched while Ron quickly walked to a side wall, took a key out of his pocket and opened a tiny safe. He emptied the contents into a paper bag along with the remaining money in the till drawer, which was sitting on the floor. There was a lot there.

'You've had a busy day,' Teddy said. 'I congratulate you.'

'And all on my own too,' Ron said, his hands shaking as he handed over the bag. Teddy thought he might burst into tears at any moment. 'I've been waiting for another member of staff for two weeks. This will serve them right.'

'Too damn right it will,' Teddy said. 'I'm going to have to tie you up now, though. Have you got any string?'

'No. But we've got some brown packing tape. How would

that be?' Ron picked up a thick roll of tape off a nearby pile of boxes.

Teddy took the offered tape and told Ron to sit down in a chair. Then he took ten minutes taping him up, arms behind his back and ankles to the chair. Ron didn't resist at all. Teddy was almost feeling sorry for him. This guy just wanted his mama.

When he'd finished he said, 'Because you've been so helpful, I'm only going to leave you here for a couple of hours, and then I'll call the police. You'll be home by midnight.'

'Fair enough.'

'But I'll have to tape your mouth. Do you have any breathing problems?'

Ron shook his head. 'Tape away.'

So Teddy put a couple of strips over his mouth, not too tightly, and left by the back door. As he headed back to his hotel he thought how that was the easiest robbery he'd ever done. Maybe he'd found his true vocation in life. He laughed out loud. The trip to Portsmouth hadn't been such a waste of time after all. Not only had he turned into a Slaphead Chameleon, but he'd come up with a bunch of money as well.

He couldn't wait to get back to his room and see just how much he'd got.

He felt he was coming up from the bottom of the ocean after spending a long time submerged. He felt heavy and sleepy like he'd been dreaming for a long time. But had he been dreaming at all? How could he remember? He couldn't remember much at all.

He could hear music, a woman's voice he recognized, a voice he liked very much. And something was touching his hand, stroking it, tickling it, almost making him laugh, although laughing would be too much of an effort. So he concentrated instead, and waited for his body to come out of the water.

As it rose slowly to the surface he remembered one thing, two words that he had to say, although they didn't make any sense at all and he didn't know why he had to say them. And then he was surfacing and he opened his eyes slowly, and through his blurred vision he saw a woman sitting there, a woman he recognized from his past. Was she the one singing? Was she the one that wanted to know his two words? He opened his mouth and said to her in a low whisper, 'Teddy Peppers.'

Then he closed his eyes and found himself sinking again.

26

Jason was reading in bed on Tuesday evening when he heard a knock on his bedroom door.

'Who is it?' he asked.

'It's me,' came Julie's reply. 'Are you decent?'

Julie came in and sat by his bed. She was wearing jeans, as she always did, and a purple V-necked T-shirt. She looked excited, like she couldn't wait to tell him something. 'Some great news. We know who the stalker is and it looks as if Jesse is getting better!'

Jason sat up and put his book aside. 'That's great! Tell me more.'

'About an hour ago Jesse came out of his coma, muttered two words and then went back to sleep. They think he's over the worst and should get better now. The two words he mentioned were "Teddy Peppers".'

'Teddy Peppers?' For some reason the name sounded familiar.

'He's an armed robber,' Julie continued. 'He was released from jail over two weeks ago and we've been looking for him in connection with a murder in Redgate. We put his photo in the papers to try to flush him out.'

Jason nodded. 'I remember now. We were in Scotland, and Jesse showed me his picture in the paper. I'm afraid he doesn't look much like my E-fit.'

'That doesn't matter now. Jesse obviously made the connection just as he was shot. He's been keeping it to himself ever since.'

'And those were the only words he spoke?'

Julie nodded. 'A true policeman.'

'A real star.' Jason felt relieved that at last they had something to go on and that Morgan was getting better. 'So what's the Gator connection?'

'Gator and Peppers were in jail together. They were lovers, apparently.'

'You're joking.'

'Quite tight, it seems.'

Jason laughed, but Julie didn't see the joke.

'So he thinks I was responsible for Gator's death, and comes to get me. Great. All I did was take in a lodger.'

'Criminals think differently to us. Revenge can take many a warped turn.'

'You're telling me. So what happens now?'

'Teddy Peppers's picture will be in the newspapers again tomorrow with the whole story so far. Hopefully that'll make him panic and he'll make his move. We'll sit tight and wait for that to happen.'

'Excuse me if I feel a bit nervous all of a sudden.'

'We'll be here all the time. We're getting another officer over as well. One at the front, one at the back and me upstairs.'

'You're not going to stay up all night, are you?'

'I'll get some sleep when the other officer turns up. In an hour or so.'

'You look a bit tired. Would you like to jump in with me?'

Julie laughed. 'Maybe when this is all over.'

Then she got up and left the room.

Jason had to think about that last remark for a while, before going back to his book.

The other officer arrived just before midnight, and Julie's heart sank when she opened the door. It was PC Garnett, the biggest chauvinist in Woodvale, a man who never looked her directly in the eye and always talked to her breasts.

Whenever she talked to him she could swear she could hear his dick move.

She let him in. She was actually taller than he was, and wondered how he'd got in the force in the first place. Surely he was under the height requirement. A bit overweight, too. She'd heard he'd had a warning recently to lose some pounds, but he was a fast-food addict and was always stuffing his face with hamburgers and chips and bars of chocolate. He also picked his nose and ate that stuff, too. On duty, standing in the street, setting a fine example. He repulsed her no end.

He had an awful grin on his face, a face that reminded her of a frog. 'Reinforcements have arrived,' he said. 'I've come to take care of you. At last I can spend the night with the lovely Julie Beech.' He laughed in his forced jovial way.

Julie grimaced. 'Yes, but luckily we'll be separated by one floor. You'll be in the kitchen. That should appeal to you.'

'Very funny.'

'But there are no burgers in there.'

She walked down the hall knowing that his eyes would be looking at her backside all the way. He followed her into the kitchen and stood a little too close. Julie took a step back.

'This is the back door, the weakest part of the downstairs. The windows aren't too strong either. There's a door down in the basement but that's got two bolts and two locks. There's no way he's coming in there unless he's got a battering ram. Hopefully you'll hear that if he does, because you're directly above it.'

Garnett snorted. He wasn't really listening to her. He was one of those types who thought he knew everything, but really knew sod all. That's why he was still a PC in his mid-thirties. He started walking around the kitchen looking in all the cupboards. Julie couldn't believe it when he looked in the fridge.

'Any food goes missing, you'll have to pay for it,' she said.

Garnett sneered at her. 'Just interested.'

She shut the fridge door and showed him the rest of the house. Brazier was in the living room, and he too groaned when he saw who'd arrived.

'Is this the best we could muster?' he said.

Garnett told him to fuck off.

Julie took him upstairs and showed him the bedrooms. He took a particular interest in hers, taking it all in. She got him out of there as quickly as possible. She didn't want to knock on Jason's door in case he was asleep, so they went back downstairs. Garnett took a chair into the kitchen and sat down right in front of the door.

'This is going to be one cushy number,' he said. 'Better than walking the streets all night.'

'Just don't fall asleep,' Julie said.

'As if.'

'I've seen it happen,' Julie said, and then she left him to it.

She went up to her room and got into Geoff's bed fully clothed, leaving her Fila trainers on the floor. The sheets had a manly smell on them, and a smell of Brut. Her father always wore the stuff so she knew the smell well. It almost made her feel at home. She closed her eyes and tried to go to sleep.

On Wednesday morning Teddy Peppers awoke in a good mood. The off-licence robbery had netted him three and a half thousand pounds! What an extra bonus that had been! He left the pub he was staying in early, and walked to Fratton station.

On the way he bought a newspaper and sat reading it on the station while awaiting his train, but felt a panic coming on when he saw a photo of himself, with a much longer article this time. Not only was the Jim Brady murder mentioned, but also the killing of Vivian and the wounding of the homeless man. But worst of all, they were now saying that the man with Vivian was a policeman who had been seriously injured but was now pulling through. Teddy couldn't believe it. A fucking copper! He'd have the whole country after him. He was glad now that he'd shaved his head, because he looked nothing like the photo they had. It was seven years old, and he was surprised to see how he'd aged since then. He'd never noticed before.

At the end of the story it said that Jason Campbell had dropped out of the Calista Shaw tour and returned home. Not exactly a subtle hint. Teddy was going back to Woodvale, anyway. He'd be there by this evening. He put the paper down and shivered.

27

When Jason went downstairs on Wednesday morning to fix his breakfast, he found a policeman in the kitchen he didn't recognize. He introduced himself as PC Garnett and had a sweaty, pudgy handshake. Jason thought he looked too unfit to be a policeman.

'So you're what all the fuss is about,' Garnett said.

'If you want to put it like that,' Jason said. 'It's not my choice, believe me.'

He started getting himself some cereal and toast and found Garnett staring at the food like a hungry dog. 'Would you like some breakfast?' he asked.

'I am a bit hungry,' Garnett said. 'I noticed you had some bacon in the fridge.'

'I could do you a bacon sandwich.'

Garnett nodded greedily. 'That would hit the spot.'

So Jason spent the next ten minutes making the odd-looking policeman a bacon sandwich. Hoad and Brazier had always brought their own food with them, and he wondered why this bloke hadn't. He also made him a cup of tea, and put plenty of tomato sauce on the bacon. Garnett was stuffing it down his throat, leaving sauce on his cheeks, when Julie came in looking rested and gorgeous. She looked at Garnett and almost recoiled at the sight.

Jason winked at her. 'I'm feeding the troops. Would you like anything?'

'Cereal would be good,' Julie said, walking past Garnett and standing with her back to him. She lowered her voice and said, 'Now you know why they call us pigs.'

The police had a plan they wanted to try, and Jason was willing to go along with it. It was to put him out in the driveway for most of the day, as if he were working on his car. This was to show Teddy Peppers that Jason was at home if he was in the vicinity, to try to force him to make his move.

So at eleven o'clock, when everyone was fed and washed, Jason drove the Nissan out of the garage and lifted up the bonnet. He was a safe distance from the road in case Peppers felt like walking past and taking a pot-shot, and Garnett was watching the back garden through the kitchen window. Julie was back upstairs in the bedroom and Officer Hoad was in the living room.

The biggest problem for Jason was how to make himself look busy. He hated working on cars, didn't know a thing about them, so after an hour of trying to look intelligent under the bonnet, he gave up and decided to wash the car instead.

He went into the kitchen, filled up a bucket and then went back outside. He started sponging the car down slowly. He had to make the job last as long as possible.

The train ride to London was uneventful, Teddy being able to relax, knowing he wouldn't have to mug anyone on the journey. With three and a half grand in his sports bag he wouldn't have to mug anyone for a while. It was a hassle he was glad to be rid of.

From Waterloo he jumped on a tube to Victoria and then on another train to Redgate. He was getting sick of all the travelling. He was glad he wasn't a touring musician.

He caught a taxi to Woodvale and asked to be dropped a hundred yards or so from Naughton Road. Then he walked along with his sports bag, trying to look nonchalant.

He was on the pavement farthest away from the house, and glancing over to his left he saw Jason Campbell washing his car. It was too obvious, he thought. It must be some kind of trap. So he kept on walking.

From the bedroom window Julie Beech saw a bald man walking past, and the hairs on the back of her neck began to rise. She picked up her Motorola personal radio and spoke to Hoad. 'I think our man may be here. A bald guy just walked past wearing a black leather jacket, carrying a sports bag.'

'What makes you think it's him?' Hoad asked. 'I thought he had white hair.'

'I had a phone call from the tour promoter earlier. A bald-headed man at the Portsmouth concert last night got irate when he learned Jason wasn't playing. He asked for a refund. He said he'd come all the way from London to see the support act. No one would do that.'

'Not unless he was a groupie.'

'Plus we know he changes his looks all the time. We have to be prepared for anyone. I've just got a gut feeling.'

'Shall I go and bring him in?'

'No. Let's just wait. But be on your toes. This might be it.'

'OK. I'll tell Garnett.'

Julie took the Glock out of her holster and waited.

Teddy walked along for a few minutes and then ducked on to the public footpath, the one that was shielded from the house by a hedge. Surely the police didn't expect him to attack Campbell in broad daylight. That would be too stupid. But they had planted him in the driveway to let him know Campbell was around, trying to force him to make a move.

He walked along the footpath back towards the house and sat on a bench to think things through. If he waited until night, which is what he'd originally planned to do, the house would be locked up and Campbell and the cops would all be inside together. He could quite easily get trapped inside, and how the hell would he get into the house anyway? He wasn't a burglar. He didn't know how to get in quietly. Once he smashed a window they'd be on him. So maybe he should just go in now, show them how a Slaphead Chameleon operated and take everyone by surprise. He could just walk up the driveway, quickly shoot or stab Campbell and then run away. Get the whole thing over with and get on with his life. So that's what he decided to do.

He looked around for a decent tree, one that would be easy to climb, and up he went with the sports bag on his shoulder. He hooked the bag over a branch and took out the flick knife. He would leave the Beretta behind this time; he hadn't had much luck with it so far. The knife would be quieter, it wouldn't alert the neighbourhood, and if the cops weren't looking out of a window he would be in and out in a silent flash. He could pick the bag up later.

He dropped to the ground and saw that the bag was well hidden. Now it was time for action.

At the bedroom window Julie was thinking that maybe she should've sent Hoad out to pick up the bald man. Her mind was working overtime worrying about it now. Had she just missed a chance to pick up Teddy Peppers? Would she get blamed for it later if someone got hurt? She felt sweat appearing on her forehead.

Teddy was on the same side of the street as the house now. He walked along the road with the knife by his side in his right hand. They wouldn't know he was there until he was right at the driveway. He could feel the excitement welling up in his body. He came to number eight and turned in.

Jason was hunched down by the side of the Nissan, cleaning the front hubcap, and only saw the man when it was too late.

He stood up and watched him approaching, a man with no hair, a curious smile on his face. Then he saw the knife in the man's right hand and knew this was it: confrontation time.

He wondered where Julie was.

He looked around but there was no one about. All he had as a weapon was a bucket of soapy water. So when the man was just about to reach him, he swung it backwards and then threw the water in the man's eyes. Then he ran off towards the back garden.

The soapy water stung Teddy's eyes and delayed him for a moment. But then he ran after Campbell. As he was passing the open kitchen door, though, a large body came out and smacked into him and they both fell against the car. Teddy managed to get the knife into the man's stomach, and pushed him away on to the ground. The man groaned and looked up at him with fear in his eyes. Teddy didn't have time to finish him off, so he ran into the back garden to look for Campbell.

Jason was in a panic as he ran across the back lawn. Where the fuck was Julie? But when he got to the back fence he saw he had something else to worry about as well.

Not being much of a gardener, he hardly ever trimmed his hedges, and he now saw that this one was far too high to jump over. The bloody thing was a colossus! He looked around for another escape route, but couldn't see one anywhere. The hedges all around were too high. He was trapped. If he got out of this alive, he promised himself to trim them all down to waist height.

But it was too late to think about that now, because here came Peppers, wet from the bucket attack, and with a bloody knife in his hand. Had he stabbed someone already? He hoped it wasn't Julie.

Jason waited for him to come. It was like one of his bad

dreams featuring the bogeyman. But he had an awful feeling that this time it was about to come true.

When the bald man had walked down the driveway, Julie had radioed the others but knew she might be too late. She swore at herself for not picking the man up earlier, and ran down the stairs. When she reached the bottom she almost crashed into Hoad as he came out of the living room. They both ran into the kitchen and out of the door, and saw Garnett lying on the ground outside, moaning.

'Stay with him,' Julie said to Hoad, and then ran into the back garden.

Jason saw Julie appear behind Peppers, but knew enough from seeing films that he shouldn't let Peppers know that she was there. So he waited for Peppers to come towards him, putting a blank expression on his face, and went into a low stance as if squaring up for a fight. Peppers just laughed at him, though, and said, 'This one's for Gator, you chicken-shit.'

Jason saw his hand come up, ready to strike, and then leaped to his right out of the way as he saw Julie raising her gun.

If you're an authorized shot, you don't have to shout a warning if you think a person's life is in danger. You have to aim at the assailant's torso and put him down.

These thoughts flashed quickly through Julie's mind, but when she saw Teddy Peppers's arm in the air, the temptation was too great. She had a score to settle with this prick, and she was damned if she was going to kill him – that would be letting him off too lightly. So she took aim at Peppers's right hand and let fly with two quick shots.

Teddy screamed as his right hand exploded. He saw two fingers fly off and land on the lawn as he crumpled to his knees in pain. He saw Campbell running away and then heard footsteps coming up behind him. Then a woman shouted at him: 'If you want your head to be next, just make a move, you fucker!'

Jason watched from a safe distance as Hoad ran over to Peppers and snapped on handcuffs, while Julie pointed the gun two-handed. He was seeing her in a new light, a new disguise, and didn't know if he liked what he saw. Then she came over and asked if he was all right. He nodded and said, 'That was some piece of shooting.'

Julie smiled in an odd way. 'That's what we're trained for. It's all part of the job.'

Jason felt as if she'd changed into someone else. She was suddenly speaking in clichés. Where was the attractive policewoman of last night, who had hinted that she might want to go to bed with him?

She took his arm and they walked out of the garden into the driveway. PC Garnett was lying there in pain, holding a handkerchief to a seeping wound. Julie stood over him and said, 'Is that blood or ketchup? That'll teach you not to smother your bacon sandwiches.'

Garnett swore at her, and Jason didn't know where to look.

28

When the police had taken Teddy Peppers away, Jason went to the kitchen and opened a bottle of white wine. He drank three glasses of it very quickly to help him relax, staring out of the window at the back lawn that had so nearly been his final place of rest.

He wondered if his house was jinxed, and if he should move out. He had nearly met his maker here twice now. Would there be other criminals coming to get revenge on him? Would a friend of Teddy Peppers now come and attack? It could be a never-ending cycle, fighting off sicko criminals for the rest of his life. Maybe he should move into a flat with a nice low mortgage, somewhere no one could find him. But he liked having a garden. Where else would he sit in the summer, drinking wine?

Julie had told him that he wouldn't be needed at the police station until the next day to make a statement, so he intended getting roaring drunk. He replayed that final scene when she came into the garden and blew Peppers's hand to pieces. That had been some shooting, and it was sweet revenge for her broken nose. But her attitude afterwards had worried him. She'd been all pumped up like some kind of female Rambo, strutting around, pushing Peppers into an ambulance. And then she'd thrown his two mangled fingers in after him, much to the amusement and disgust of the other policemen on the scene. The fingers had no chance of being sewn back on; she had just been getting her own back even more.

Jason obviously didn't know Julie well at all, didn't know

anything about police work or the effect it could have on a person. He'd been seeing her as some kind of fantasy figure, Teri Hatcher coming off the TV screen to visit him in Woodvale. What an idiot he'd been! A typical male reaction, only seeing her looks and not the person underneath. Well, he'd made that mistake before, and was bound to make it again.

He took his bottle of wine into the basement and played his electric piano for an hour. He played Dylan's 'I Want You' one last time to signify the end of his longing for Julie. What a strange month it had been. First the tour had perked him up, then Teddy Peppers had brought him back down, then Julie had brought him both up *and* down. What else was in store?

Feeling nicely buzzed when all the wine was gone, Jason went upstairs to the living room and rang Charles Penn at the Reivers Agency. He told him he was ready to tour again and would like to resume with the Norwich concert. That would leave him just the last four: Norwich, Cambridge, Coventry and Leeds. Penn said that would be fine. It would give Jason a week to get his head together and come back refreshed.

Jason put the phone down and went to the kitchen for another bottle of wine. As he drank his first glass he thought about his lodgers. He would have to ring and tell them it was safe to return home. But he could do all that tomorrow. For now he was just going to drown himself in drink.

They took him to the hospital first, sitting in between two oversized policemen in a slow-moving ambulance, his hand in agony, his two mangled fingers lying in a waste bin. Teddy was finding it hard to think clearly, so many things were racing through his head. He was cursing himself, mainly, for going in after Campbell in broad daylight. It had seemed like a good idea at the time, but in retrospect was pretty foolish. How many cops had been in the house? Three? How could he have expected to take on three cops and Campbell? Well, at least he'd managed to stab one of them.

He had now wounded two policemen, one homeless waster, killed Vivian and Jim Brady and attempted to murder Campbell. An impressive list of destruction, and they'd be throwing the book at him this time, although he wouldn't admit to the Brady killing until they proved it.

He could now look forward to the rest of his days inside. There was no way they would let him out until he was well into his seventies, an old fart walking around with a Zimmer frame. Jesus Christ! What a lot he had to look forward to. He had only been out of jail just under three weeks.

He thought of his sports bag, which was still hanging from the tree in Naughton Road. He tried to imagine someone finding it in a few months' time; some kid going climbing, finding the richest treasure he would ever come across. It made Teddy smile. He wouldn't mind some kid finding it and putting it to use. As long as the cops didn't get it.

The ambulance arrived at the hospital and Teddy was marched into casualty and stuck in a private room to await a doctor. One of the policemen stayed with him, and there was another keeping watch outside. There was no way of escaping. Besides, he wanted to get his hand fixed first; it hurt like hell.

He lay down on the bed thinking how much he'd like to come face to face with the bitch who had shot him. It was the one whose nose he'd broken. He had recognized her as she was being led away, and then she'd thrown his fingers at him. What a cow! He'd like to pay her back for that.

He didn't realize they let policewomen fire guns these days as well. What was the world coming to? But it was a great piece of shooting, even he had to admit. He closed his eyes and tried to shut out the pain. He wondered if this really was the end of the road. Keep positive, he thought. Something might turn up.

They questioned him that evening, back in Woodvale police station, his hand all bandaged now, but still with a dull ache. There were two of them, and they gave him a really hard time.

One was a red-headed Scotsman called Kiddie, who looked like he would hit him if they were left alone together, and the other was called Hickle, who was calmer but looked just as tough.

The policeman he had shot in Preston was their close buddy Detective Inspector Morgan and they seemed intent on getting justice mainly for him. They didn't seem to care too much about Vivian or even the other cop, Garnett, and they had nothing on him for the Brady murder, so he just played dumb on that one. Sitting next to him throughout was a solicitor called Leeder, but it didn't make much difference in the scheme of things.

Back in his cell afterwards he thought about his bleak prospects and couldn't come to terms with them. He also cursed the outfit they had him wearing, an all-white job that all prisoners ended up in while they were being held. He felt anonymous, like he was wearing a pair of pyjamas. He longed for some of the clothes he'd been buying recently, especially his black leather jacket. But they were all back in the sports bag, up in the tree, waiting for some kid to find them.

'So what do you think?' Kiddie asked Hickle. They were sitting opposite each other in the interview room, arms leaning on the table between them. It reminded Kiddie of one of those Smith and Jones comedy routines on TV.

'I think he's a slimy character who's trying to pull one over on us,' Hickle said.

'Like what?'

'Like the Brady murder.'

'You really think he did that one as well?'

'Who else could it have been?'

'I don't know.'

'He comes out of prison, and goes to see Brady straight away; the man who took over his wife and kids as soon as he was in jail. He probably asked him for money to tide him over. Brady refused, and got hit over the head for it. It wasn't a premeditated murder. He just picked up a bit of wood and hit him.'

'Don't you think it's a bit of a coincidence?' Kiddie asked.

'What's a coincidence?'

'That Brady was murdered in Redgate, and Campbell, the man he comes to get revenge on, only lives down the road in Woodvale. Seems a bit convenient to me.'

'But that's the whole point.'

'How do you mean?'

'Peppers's first concern on coming out of prison was to get Campbell. But then he realized that Woodvale is only about five miles from Horley where his ex lives. So he thinks, I may as well pay Jim Brady a visit too, while I'm in the area. Even more convenient is that Brady only works a few miles from where Campbell lives. The Brady murder is just bad luck. If he'd been living farther away I don't think Peppers would have gone for him. He was just chancing his arm. That's what he is. A chancer.'

Kiddie puffed out his cheeks. 'That almost makes it worse. Oh, I'm just in the area, so I'll do this bloke at the same time.'

'Exactly. He's a nutter. Who else would've tried attacking Campbell at his house in broad daylight, knowing there must've been some cops in there? He was chancing it again. It's all part of his character.'

'But there's nothing we can do about the Brady murder unless he admits it. Forensics didn't come up with anything. They still haven't found the piece of wood. It's disappeared into thin air.'

'That's what's so annoying. You'd think they'd turn up something. That's what they're paid for.'

'Maybe they could make something up. Or we could make something up. Just to get him to admit it.'

'It's worth thinking about. We'll give him another go later. Try and wear him down.'

'At least we've got him on a lot of other stuff. He'll never drink a pint of beer as a free man again.'

'That's right. But I don't like loose ends. I like things to be cleaned up.'

'Everyone likes a clean slate.'

'Or a clean plate. Shall we go to the canteen?'

They left the interview room and walked down the corridor.

'When's Jesse coming home?' Hickle asked.

'In a few days. His ex will be driving him down.'

'Is he going to come back to work?'

'I wouldn't think so. He's not well enough yet, and I don't think it'll be worth it after that. As far as I'm concerned that's the last we'll see of him here.'

'A pity. He'll be a hard act to follow.'

'I'm going to miss him a lot,' Kiddie said.

They went into the canteen and picked up an empty tray each.

29

Jason carried on drinking on Thursday too. And Friday as well. He still hadn't telephoned his lodgers to tell them to come home. He needed his own space, and didn't want to have to explain anything to anyone. The shock of seeing a knife coming towards him was just starting to sink in. He was also thinking about his life in more detail, where it was going, and what he was going to do.

He had been to the police station yesterday morning and given a lengthy statement. They had told him he'd be needed in court later in the year, or early next year, when the case came to trial. He hadn't thought about that. He would have to face Teddy Peppers again. He wasn't filled with joy at the thought.

He was halfway through his second bottle of wine by midday when the front doorbell rang. He left the living room where he had been sitting staring at the walls, and went to answer it. He found Julie standing there, and let her in. 'You look tired,' he said. 'Would you like a drink?'

'You look like you've had a few already.'

'More than that.'

'I may as well join you.'

He went to the kitchen to fetch another glass and then they went into the living room. They sat next to each other on the sofa, and Julie told him she'd been given a week off.

'I had a debriefing yesterday,' she said. 'They've got a big problem with my shooting.'

'Why? It was a fine piece of marksmanship.'

'According to them it wasn't. In a situation like that I'm

meant to aim at the torso. I should've killed him, not aimed to wound.'

'It would've saved the taxpayer a lot of money.'

'They're saying I endangered your life. If I'd missed his hand there's a chance he would've stabbed you. I told them that was rubbish. If he'd attacked you I would've shot him in the back.'

'But he was attacking me.'

'Yes, but I knew what I was doing. I knew I wouldn't miss. I'm a great shot. If I'd shot him in the back he never would have known it was me who got him. I wanted to give him something to remind him of me. Every time he plays with himself he'll be thinking of me.'

Jason laughed. 'He certainly will. It'll never be the same again.' He liked the way Julie was today, not as gung-ho as she had been on Wednesday.

'So the outcome may be that I lose my right to be an authorized shot. Everything I've trained for out of the window because I chose to wound someone instead of killing them. Does that make sense to you?'

Jason shook his head. 'Not really. But then a lot of what's happened hasn't made a lot of sense to me. I'm just a singer, and I get mixed up in all this.'

'They even asked me if I needed counselling. Someone to talk things over with.'

'And what did you say?'

'I said no thanks. I told them I felt great about shooting someone who's disfigured me for life. They didn't know what to say to that.'

'You tell them.'

'It's all been very strange. I need to get drunk.' She picked up her glass and took a sip. 'Why is white wine called white wine?' she said. 'It's yellow. It should be called yellow wine.'

Jason smiled. 'You know I prefer you like this. I didn't like you when you had a gun in your hand.'

'I'm not sure I liked me either. I'm a bit confused. I don't know what I need any more.'

'I need to get laid,' Jason said. 'How about you?'

Julie smiled at him. 'Don't be subtle, or anything.'

'I haven't time for being subtle any more. Who knows when I may get knifed?' He reached over and took her hand and she slid next to him. He put his arm around her.

'Are your lodgers in?' she asked.

'I haven't told them to come back yet. I'm enjoying my freedom.'

'Then what are we waiting for?' she said. She reached for his glasses, took them off his nose and put them on the table.

They lay naked together in Jason's single bed, far too small for two people. He had always meant to get a double but hadn't had a serious relationship since Heather left four years ago, just a few quick flings, so what was the point?

He wondered if this was going to be a quick fling. It had certainly been very enjoyable, and Julie had a great body. Athletic and slim, breasts that were bigger than he'd imagined. He wondered what she'd thought of his body: forty-one years old and out of shape, with a gut he couldn't get rid of that was spreading because he was drinking too much. He felt her hand running over it now, playing with the hairs on his stomach.

'I've never slept with a man with a beer belly before,' she said, as if reading his mind.

'I'm sure you'll find a lot more as you get older,' he said, jumping to the defence of his thickening waistline.

'That's something to look forward to.'

He turned to kiss her and ran his tongue over her broken nose. He didn't mind it at all.

'I feel a lot better than I did an hour ago,' he said.

'Me too. It helps get rid of the tension.'

'We should do it more often.'

'Ready when you are.'

'Would you like to hear something first?'

'What's that?'

'I started writing a song for you.'

'Let's hear it, then.'

'I'll just tell you the first verse, as all my guitars are downstairs.'

'OK.'

'It's called "No Matter Where I Go". "No matter where I go, she's always on my mind. No matter where I roam, she's always close behind. And I see her on the street, and I see her on a train. No matter where I go, I'll see her once again."'

'Is that it?'

'That's one verse. Want to hear another?'

'OK.'

'"I've always been the kind, who'll hang on to a dream. Some people call me blind, but they're just being mean. And it's far too late to change, I'm all set in my ways. I've always been the kind, who'll wait for days and days."'

'That's nice,' Julie said. 'Can I hear the tune sometime?'

'I'm still working on it, but I'll let you know when it's ready.'

She leaned over and kissed him. 'Can we do something else now?'

'Sure.'

'I'd like my toes sucked this time.'

'Pardon?'

'I'd like my toes sucked. I'm an unusual girl.'

'You can say that again.'

But Jason did as he was told.

In Margaret Ward in the Sharoe Green Hospital, Jesse Morgan was sitting up in bed eating a regular meal like a regular man.

He had been in a coma for a week altogether, until that fateful evening on Tuesday when he'd risen from his dreams and muttered the name of Teddy Peppers. That was three days ago now, and he was getting stronger each day. The doctors had told him he could leave hospital next week. Either Wednesday or Thursday.

The door to his room opened and Nicola came in carrying a bunch of flowers.

'I know you're not a flower man,' she said, 'but this place needs brightening up.' She came over and kissed him on the lips.

'It brightens every time you walk in,' Morgan said.

'Keep flattering and I might have to climb in there with you.'

'That's what I'm counting on.'

He watched as Nicola found an empty vase, filled it at the sink and arranged the flowers. 'How was the drive?' he asked.

'Long and tedious. Will motorway driving ever be interesting?'

'Not in this lifetime.'

'You're lucky still to be in this lifetime.'

'Not really. Have you heard of the saying, "Not dead, only resting"?'

Nicola shook her head.

'I can't remember who said it. Maybe it was a book I read or something. But that's what I was doing. I was just having a long rest.'

Nicola placed the flowers on his bedside table and pulled up a chair. This was her second visit to Preston in a week. After he'd woken up on Tuesday she had driven back to Woodvale the next day, and now here she was again for a weekend visit. He felt very touched by her concern, and wondered if maybe this was the time to start talking again about their relationship. Or maybe not. It could probably wait until he was well again and back down in Woodvale.

'How did you work that one out?' Nicola asked, taking his hand in hers.

'I was talking to the doctor this morning. I had one bullet

that clipped my head, one that entered my thigh and one that grazed my stomach. He said I shouldn't have gone into a coma for those kind of injuries, and that maybe it was self-induced.'

'A self-induced coma? I've never heard of such a thing.'

'Neither have I, but then again I'm not a medical man. He said maybe I just wanted some time to rest and think about things. Take some time out.'

'Sounds crazy to me.'

'Well, not so crazy. I've been pretty depressed over the past few weeks. Mainly because of Aidan Pearson's death. He reckoned that maybe I just wanted to hide away for a while and think things through.'

'But you weren't thinking while you were in a coma, were you?'

'Not that I remember, but then how did I come up with Teddy Peppers's name? There must have been something going on in my head.'

Nicola nodded. 'There's usually too much going on in your head. That's always been your problem.'

Morgan decided to let that one pass. 'Have you got any gossip for me? Did they get Teddy Peppers yet?'

'You've been missing all the fun. Ian Kiddie came into the pub yesterday and told me everything. It's been quite exciting, really.'

'Tell me more.'

So Morgan finished his meal and listened as Nicola told him about the shooting at Naughton Road. She told him how Julie Beech was in trouble now for not killing Peppers outright, and how Jason was soon going back on tour. She also said how they thought Peppers had been responsible for the killing of Jim Brady at Bell's Plastics factory, although they still didn't have any evidence. Morgan had forgotten all about that murder.

'Can you take this tray for me?' he asked, when she'd finished.

Nicola took the tray and placed it on a table.

'You can have a meal too, if you like,' Morgan said. 'Or an ice cream.'

'No thanks.' She sat back down next to him and took his hand again.

'I forgot to thank you about the music,' he said.

'What music?'

'The Calista Shaw CD. The one I woke up to.'

Nicola smiled. 'I knew you wouldn't wake up to Garth Brooks. Or Daniel O'Donnell.'

'Kiddie was playing Daniel O'Donnell? Jesus. No wonder I was out for a week.'

Nicola reached down and pulled a carrier bag on to her lap.

'I brought the electric razor you wanted,' she said. 'I didn't know you had one.'

'I use it to trim my beard. A useful object.'

'Have you decided what you want?'

'I want all my hair shaved off and the sides of my beard. I want you to leave me with just a goatee.'

'Isn't that a bit drastic?'

'I'm not going to walk around with a hole in my hair. I may as well start afresh.'

The doctors had shaved away a big portion of Morgan's hair when they were repairing his scalp wound. He felt he would rather be bald for a while rather than have a big hole. And he'd have to shave his beard to a goatee because a full beard with no hair would look ridiculous.

'Do you want to do it now?' Nicola asked.

'No time like the present. It'll give my hair a few days to grow back before I get out.'

'What if it doesn't grow back?'

'Then I'll come looking for you.'

Nicola stood up and plugged in the razor.

30

The weekend went slowly for Teddy Peppers, sitting in his cell at Woodvale police station, awaiting a transfer on Monday to Wormwood Scrubs. On Friday he had appeared in a magistrates' court and been charged with Vivian's murder, along with the attempted murder of the two policemen and Jason Campbell, and the wounding of the homeless man.

Once in Wormwood Scrubs, Teddy would then have a long wait before his trial came around, a wait he wasn't looking forward to. He had heard many bad stories about the Scrubs, particularly about the screws, who were getting a reputation for violence against prisoners. Apparently they took two-hour lunch breaks, came back pissed, then beat the shit out of anyone who blinked. Well, Teddy wasn't going to stand for that. He'd have nothing to lose by hitting back at a few of them.

He tried to block it out of his mind as he sat in his cell reading the second book of his stay.

The first book he'd read, courtesy of the custody sergeant, had been called *One Day in the Life of Ivan Denisovich* by a Russian writer called Alexander Solz . . . Teddy couldn't pronounce the rest of his name. It seems this Solzy guy was locked up in a Siberian prison camp a long time ago and had written all about it. The terrible conditions almost made Teddy feel he was living in a holiday camp, and he'd devoured the short book quite quickly, for him.

Now he was slogging his way through another Russian writer, another name he couldn't pronounce, so Teddy had christened him Dusty Fido. The book was called *Crime and Punishment* and was all about a cat-and-mouse game between a murderer and a police inspector. Teddy sympathized strongly with the murderer, and was hoping he'd get away in the end, but didn't hold out too much hope. He wondered how many other criminals had read these books in these cells – both copies were nearly falling apart – and if they'd been given to him intentionally in the hope of maybe changing his outlook on life. Well, Teddy didn't mind reading to kill some time, but he was buggered if he'd let some book change the way he thought. He yawned and stretched in his white pyjama outfit.

Teddy had never known a police station as quiet as this one. A few drunks had been brought in on Saturday evening, but apart from that he'd been the only one in the whole cell block. Today was his fourth day in there, and he was trying to divide his days into some kind of routine to make them go quicker. In the mornings he would read the *Daily Mirror* they gave him from cover to cover, and in the afternoons he would read his paperback. He would try to make his meals last as long as possible, but there were only so many times you could chew a piece of meat, or suck on a sandwich until it was a pulp.

His right hand was still causing him pain, and a doctor came to see him every other day. They told him that if it hadn't been for his injury he'd be in the Scrubs already, as if he should be grateful.

On the second night in his cell, after reminiscing about his sex sessions with Vivian, he had tried having a wank but it had been impossible with a bandaged hand, so he had tried using his left. He knew there was a school of thought that said if you wank with your left hand it's more exciting because it feels as though someone else is doing it, but Teddy had never been convinced by that theory. He found it very clumsy using his wrong hand, although he did eventually manage a pathetic little squirt. After that he gave up.

He'd remain celibate until his hand was properly healed. Then he'd try again.

Jason's relationship with Julie had turned into a sex-filled weekend, and after he'd rung his two lodgers to tell them to come home, he transferred his passions to Julie's flat.

It was situated in a small block of nine, an unusual building between Woodvale and Redgate that Jason had never noticed before. It was in a quiet residential area, next to some bungalows, not far from the hospital where Jason's broken thumb had been mended in 1995. There was a small gravel parking area at the front, and then the square grey block of flats behind it. Julie had bought hers for £45,000 just under a year ago, and she was on the second floor up a clean flight of stairs. The inside was quite small, rectangular in shape, but it was very modern and ideal for a person living alone. When you walked in the front door the bedroom was on the right, then a bathroom, then the kitchen and a good-sized living room. Julie didn't have many possessions, so the rooms were uncluttered. The bedroom had fitted wardrobes, and, most importantly, a double bed, which took up most of the floor space. They spent most of their time in there.

It got Jason thinking that maybe he should sell his house and buy somewhere like this instead. The mortgage would be almost half what he was paying now, and he could go back to living on his own. But then he thought of all his instruments and electrical gear. Where the hell would he keep those? And what about all the noise he was used to making? He wouldn't be able to play amplified instruments in a flat.

'Don't you need to go home and practise?' Julie asked him on Sunday evening. They were lying in the double bed reading stacks of newspapers.

'Are you trying to get rid of me?'

'No. I could do with some more sex first. But you'll be

going back on tour soon. Don't you need to prepare?'

'I've got until Tuesday. I'll go home tomorrow.'

'OK.'

'I should be able to do them on autopilot anyway. All the rehearsing's already been done. Are you going to come to any of the shows?'

'Maybe Cambridge. How would that be? It wouldn't take long to drive there.'

'Sounds good to me. It's Norwich, Tuesday night. I'll drive there on my own. Cambridge is meant to be a nice venue.'

'I've never even been there. Would you believe it?'

'You're too wrapped up in your police work. And see where it's got you. A suspension for doing your job properly.'

'I may have to change my priorities.'

'I may have to change mine, too. I quite fancy a flat like this.'

'You'll never get rid of your house. You love it too much.'

'Want to bet?'

'No.' Julie put down the newspaper and folded it neatly. 'Are you ready for that sex yet?'

Jason dropped his newspaper on the floor. 'What position shall we try this time?'

It was early Monday morning when they came to move Teddy Peppers. The doctor gave his hand a final look, and by now Teddy was quite glad to be pronounced fit enough for Wormwood Scrubs. He wanted to talk to some other criminals and get away from Russian novels.

He was still dressed all in white as they led him out, and they had given him a white pair of plimsolls as well. The trainers and clothes he'd been wearing when he'd been caught were being held as evidence. He was leaving empty-handed.

He was handcuffed to a policeman and another walked along beside them. They led him down a corridor and into the backyard, where they kept all the vehicles.

'It's a nice day for it,' the policeman handcuffed to him said, breathing in the fresh air. It was quite warm for October.

'A nice day for what?' Teddy asked.

'For a ride in a van. All the way to sunny Scrubs.'

Teddy looked around the yard but could only see police cars. 'Where is the van?' he asked.

'They'll be here in a minute,' the policeman said.

Teddy nodded. Something didn't feel right.

The other policeman stepped up to him and said, 'We've got a few minutes to kill. What shall we do?' He had an ugly, pock-marked face and was in his forties.

'Fuck knows,' Teddy said. 'Do what you want.' He looked him in the eye and guessed what was coming next. He was surprised they'd waited this long.

The policeman hit him in the stomach and Teddy bent over double, the breath rushing out of him. He would have fallen to the ground if he hadn't been handcuffed to the other bastard.

'That one's for Jesse Morgan,' the policeman said.

He lifted Teddy by the throat and pushed him against the wall. 'And this one's for Julie Beech.' He punched him hard in the ribs, and that hurt even more. Teddy felt as if he were going to be sick, which wouldn't be such a bad thing in the circumstances, because he quite fancied puking all over the arsehole.

'And this one's for Garnett,' the policeman said.

Teddy tensed himself for the next blow, but there was the sound of a vehicle approaching and the policeman didn't have time to land it. He remained hunched over while the other policeman tried holding him up. He heard the vehicle stop close by and then sensed someone else walking towards them.

'What's wrong with him?' a voice asked.

'He's got gut ache,' the pock-marked policeman said. 'But he should be OK. I don't think he'll puke in your van or anything.'

'He'd better not. I only just cleaned it.'

They pushed him towards the van, still in a crouch, still hurting, not looking up. Teddy wished he had his knife on him so he could stick one of them before he left.

When he was next to the van he stood up straight, his stomach already stiffening, feeling angry and miserable. He looked with puzzlement at the sign painted on the side. It said Seven Securitas, and he felt his spirits starting to lift.

31

They put him in the back of the van with his handcuffs on and shut the door. Then it started up and pulled slowly away from the police station.

Teddy moved to the back and looked out of the small window. He trawled through his brain for things that had happened in the last year or two, but couldn't really remember too much. He tried to think harder.

What he did know was that Seven Securitas had hit the headlines more than once either this year or last, for letting criminals escape from their vans when they were being transported to prisons. Teddy couldn't remember the details exactly, but the escapes had happened in quick succession and the security firm had become a national laughing stock. He could recall comedians on TV telling jokes about them, wondering why they had been given the task in the first place. But their record had improved slightly since, and they obviously still had the contract.

He wondered how the criminals had got away. Had they made a run for it when a door had been left open? Had someone set them free? He was pretty sure they'd all been recaptured and that it hadn't reoccurred for a while, but still, it was a ray a light on an otherwise gloomy horizon, and maybe something lucky would happen before they got to Wormwood Scrubs. He leaned back on the metal bench and rubbed his ribs, trying to get rid of the pain.

He felt a little better the longer the journey went on. He was content looking out of the back window, thinking of a way to escape.

They were in the London suburbs now, driving slower, getting stuck in traffic jams. He tried the door handle but nothing was shifting there. He knew these vans were tough things to get into from the days he'd been trying to rob them. His gang always waited for the money to come outside with a security guard, rather than try getting inside a van. Only a madman would use that method. He had noticed that this one had a combination lock on the door, so there was no way out from the inside. He would have to wait for something else to happen.

Eventually the van turned down a narrow street and came to a stop, and when Teddy looked out of the window they were at another police station. He didn't think they were at the Scrubs yet, so where the hell were they?

About five minutes later the back doors opened, and while Teddy was thinking of diving out, another man was pushed in and the doors shut quickly behind him. They said hello to each other as the man sat down opposite, and Teddy introduced himself.

'Just call me Mr Muscle,' the other man said. 'Maybe you've heard of me?'

Teddy shook his head. 'Can't say that I have. Where the hell are we, anyway?'

'Croydon,' Mr Muscle said. 'Where did you get on?'

'A shithole called Woodvale. You probably haven't heard of it.'

'Doesn't ring any bells,' Mr Muscle said.

He looked to be in his thirties, a stocky man with broad shoulders, cropped hair and a suntan. His face was round and he had a broken nose and piggy eyes. Even Teddy found him a bit scary. 'So why do they call you Mr Muscle?' he asked.

The other man smiled. 'After the kitchen cleaner. The last time I was inside I used to work in the kitchens. Cleaning dishes and cooking surfaces. I always used to have a squirty gun of Mr Muscle in my hand. You know the stuff?'

'In a plastic bottle with an orange gun?'

'That's the one. Well, that's what they called me inside. It fit quite well, especially when I came out. I gave up armed robbery and starting shooting people for a living. Mr Muscle: for killing germs and scum; does the jobs that no one else wants to do.' He smiled again, obviously very proud of his name.

Teddy nodded. 'My name's a bit like that too. I'm known as the Slaphead Chameleon, because I can change my appearance and slink away to safety.'

'That's an unusual name. Has a certain ring to it.'

'I like it,' Teddy admitted.

'But you obviously didn't slink away this time. What have they got you for?'

'Just about everything at the moment,' Teddy said, then proceeded to outline his three weeks of destruction since leaving jail. It was an impressive list.

'What happened to your hand?' Mr Muscle asked.

'The policewoman whose nose I broke got her own back. Shot two of my digits off.'

'What a bitch.'

'Yeah, I'd like to meet her again. What bugs me most, though, is I've got three and a half grand sitting in a sports bag down in Woodvale waiting to be picked up. And I can't get my fucking hands on it.'

Mr Muscle lapsed into silence. Teddy looked out of the window, wondering how close they were to the Scrubs.

'Well, there is a way around this,' Mr Muscle said. 'If you're interested.'

'Too right I'm interested,' Teddy said. 'Fire away.'

'Well, just before we get to the Scrubs I'm getting sprung from this tin can. The doors will be wide open for a few seconds. I can't take you with me, but you can join me later if you need work. The three and a half grand will buy you in.'

Teddy couldn't believe what he was hearing. There was a God after all! 'How the hell are you going to get out of here?' he asked.

'That doesn't matter. The less you know the better. But sometime soon that door will pop open and out we go.'

'I can't believe it. It must be my lucky day.'

'Maybe it is. But that's your big chance. Just run for it. I'm getting picked up, so don't go the same way as me. If you want a job, just go to The Porter's Arms in Clapham when you can. Ask for me. I can always be reached there.'

'I will,' Teddy said. 'I don't know what to say. I'd almost given up hope.'

'Think nothing of it. Us criminals have to stick together.'

Teddy nodded. 'You must be important for someone to go to this amount of trouble.'

Mr Muscle tapped the side of his nose. 'It's not what you know, it's who you know.'

Teddy smiled. 'Do we just sit and wait for it to happen?'

'That's about it. But while we're waiting . . .' He reached down to his left trainer, undid the laces and slid his foot out. A small piece of bent metal fell on to the floor. A burglar's lock pick. 'Let's see if we can get these handcuffs off,' he said.

For the next twenty minutes they took turns with the lock pick, Mr Muscle showing Teddy what to do, until both sets of handcuffs lay on the floor.

'Amazing,' Teddy said, rubbing his wrists.

'Just another trick of the trade.'

They sat in silence for a while, and Teddy got more and more tense. He still couldn't believe this was happening. He tucked in his white shirt so it wouldn't look so much like a pair of pyjamas. He was going to stand out, all in white, but that was a minor inconvenience. He looked at Mr Muscle sitting there calmly as if this were an everyday occurrence. Maybe it was. 'What's it like being a hit man?' he asked.

'Short hours, good pay,' Mr Muscle said. 'If you work for the right people.'

'Did you ever see that film called *Grosse Pointe Blank*? About a hit man?'

Mr Muscle nodded. 'What a load of shite.'

'I'm glad you thought that,' Teddy said.

He was about to say more when there was a soft sound at the doors.

Then a few seconds later they popped open.

Teddy didn't have time to say goodbye or thank you; Mr Muscle was already gone. He'd jumped to the right, so Teddy jumped to the left.

The van had been stuck in a traffic jam when the door had opened, so Teddy just walked through the cars and crossed the road. It was a busy shopping day, wherever they were.

He walked down the street at pace and entered the first large store he came to, a Littlewoods. He walked quickly across the ground floor and exited from a door on the other side. As he carried on walking, he knew that people were looking at his all-white clothes. Who wore all white in October? If it had been midsummer he wouldn't have stood out so much. He was worrying mostly about his trousers. The crotch was very low, hanging almost to his knees, but the more he walked, the more youngsters he saw wearing jeans in the same low-slung-crotch fashion. They too looked ridiculous, so hell, it must be the latest thing. Teddy relaxed a little, but still wanted to get rid of the shirt.

He ducked down a seedy alleyway and walked along until he found a tramp, a middle-aged man sitting on the ground drinking from a bottle of cider. Teddy bent down in front of him and socked him on the jaw before he could say anything. Then he laid him flat on the ground and started stripping off his dirty coat, which stank of booze and piss. It was a long brown job of the mac variety, and would've been perfect if it was cleaner. Teddy decided to keep the shirt on for protection, and waved the coat around in the air a few times to see if it would improve matters. It didn't, but a few coins fell out of the pockets, so he picked them up and then went through the man's trousers to see if there were any more. He managed to scrounge ninety-five pence.

He left the alleyway with the coat buttoned around him. He stank to high heaven, but at least he wasn't the man in white any more. He tried to leave the smell behind him by walking a little faster.

He went back to the main road and tried to figure out which way to go. He asked an old woman which direction New Cross was, and she almost fainted in front of him. She held up a seventy-year-old arm and said, 'That way!'

Teddy walked in the recommended direction until he came to a bus stop. He looked at the timetable, saw New Cross listed there and waited for a 53 to come along. He stood away from the queue next to a shop, so people wouldn't have to smell him.

It only took five minutes for a 53 to appear, but it felt like longer. Teddy was listening for sirens but didn't hear anything.

He stepped into the queue and listened to the amounts of money people were handing over to the driver. He was worried about ninety-five pence not being enough, but as he got nearer he heard someone asking for a seventy-pence ticket, so he knew he'd be all right. When his turn came he said the same thing, and the driver gave him a suspicious look. Luckily he was behind a glass divider, so probably couldn't smell him too much.

Teddy took the ticket and pushed his way upstairs. One good thing about smelling was that people moved out of his way. The bus lurched into action as he made his way towards the back. He almost fell over, but managed to find an empty seat and sat down. He breathed a sigh of relief and looked out of the window. He saw two cops standing there talking into their radios, looking up and down the street. Teddy wiped the sweat off his bald head. He was a free man once again.

32

The doorbell rang at number eight Naughton Road.

Jason swore and stopped mid-song. He put down his guitar and walked up the basement steps. When he opened the door Julie was standing there looking flustered.

'Teddy Peppers has just escaped,' she said. 'You'd better pack your things and come with me.'

Jason wasn't sure if he'd heard right. 'Can you say that again?'

Julie stepped in through the door and looked behind her before shutting it. Jason had never seen her so angry. 'Those fools at Seven Securitas. They were transferring him to Wormwood Scrubs and somehow he got away. Him and another criminal.'

'What? Escaped from a security van?'

'It's all a fucking joke! Why do I bother? I catch the bastard and then they let him get away. I give up!'

She walked past him into the living room. When he joined her she was pacing up and down, looking even more agitated.

'Would you like a drink?' he asked.

'No thanks. A machine gun would be handy, though.'

He sat down on the sofa and waited for her to unwind. She strutted some more and swore. 'So what happens now?' he asked.

'You pack up your things and come with me. You can stay at my place until we decide what to do. Bring your guitars and all your tour stuff.'

'You really think he'll come after me again? Don't you

think he's learned his lesson? He's probably just grateful to be free.'

'You can never trust a psycho. He'll be totally unpredictable. We have to prepare for anything.'

'I thought you were suspended, anyway?'

'I'm miraculously back on duty. They rang me and told me to come over. They said I should stay with you until further notice.'

'Did they give you your gun back as well?'

'That's the downside. They said there was no way I could be armed until the inquiry's over.'

'Well that's fucking great. What's the point of that?'

Julie held up her hands. 'I don't know any more. None of it makes sense.'

She looked like she might burst into tears, so Jason stood up and took her in his arms. He held her for a while and stroked her hair. 'Don't worry. I'm sure it'll all turn out OK.'

He wondered if he sounded convincing, because he sure as hell didn't feel it.

Teddy Peppers was standing under a nice hot shower, washing away the smell of the awful mac. He was back in the flat of Stacey, the young woman he had picked up and slept with on his London interlude before the Queen Elizabeth Hall fiasco.

After jumping off the bus at New Cross railway station, he had retraced the route to Stacey's flat and rung the front doorbell. There had been no reply, which wasn't surprising because she was a working girl. He had sworn out loud and marched off looking for a park, where, for the rest of the day, he had pretended to be a down-and-out. He had sat on a bench for a while but was too noticeable, so he had walked into a clump of bushes and hidden in there. He had lain down on the dirt and tried to sleep, but it was a bit too cold for that. Later on it had started to drizzle, so he had sat there hunched in a ball. He hadn't felt too miserable, though, because he was still so grateful to be free. He had done a lot of thinking, planning his next move.

He didn't have a watch on, so he had stayed there until it started getting dark and had then gone back to Stacey's. She answered his ring this time, but turned up her nose when she saw him. She didn't recognize him at first with his bald head, but he managed to persuade her to let him in. He took the coat off straight away and stuffed it in the rubbish bin. Then he told her the story he'd concocted in the bushes.

He told her he'd been on a wild bender with his mates the night before, and hadn't been able to get home. He had caught the wrong night bus and ended up in New Cross without any money. He'd borrowed a coat from a down-and-out and spent the night sleeping in a park. He'd missed her in the morning, so had waited all day for her return.

What about the clothes? she had asked. Why are you all dressed up in white? Teddy had told her he'd been to a fancy-dress party as well, dressed as a sailor. He didn't know how he'd managed to say that without cracking up. His reply hung in the air for a few moments while Stacey stood and wondered if he was telling the truth. And what about his bandaged hand? Teddy said he'd cut it at the party. Then Stacey smiled and said he'd better get in the shower. Teddy couldn't get in there quick enough.

Afterwards, he asked Stacey if she had some clothes he could borrow. All her jeans were too tight, so he had to make do with a pair of black leggings. Stacey found that quite a laugh, but soon shut up when Teddy gave her a dirty look. He studied himself in the mirror. He looked like a poncey ballet dancer, but it would have to do. Then Stacey gave him an old Winnie-the-Pooh T-shirt, and a Christmas-present jumper she had never worn which had a moose on the front. Teddy studied himself again. He looked a right state. He had bare ankles between the leggings and his plimsolls, and his balls looked like a sack of onions. He'd probably get arrested for indecent exposure. He asked Stacey if she had a coat he could wear, but she shook her head. Then she told him with a straight face that he didn't have to bring the clothes back.

Teddy said he had to go. He asked if he could borrow ten pounds as well, and Stacey coughed up with no resistance; he sensed she was quite relieved to see the back of him. Then he walked out with the prison whites rolled up under his arm, saying he would have to return them to the fancy-dress hire shop tomorrow.

He walked down to the station and tossed the whites into a bin along the way. He passed a few schoolgirls and they sniggered at him. He bought a train ticket to Charing Cross and then jumped on the tube, taking the short ride to Victoria station. People kept looking at his stupid outfit, and he wondered whether he should turn the jumper inside out. He couldn't be bothered. To hell with them.

At Victoria he bought a single ticket to Redgate, and then his money was virtually gone. He would have to walk all the way from Redgate to Woodvale, which would be a bit of a drag, but it would be worth it because of the prize awaiting him. He couldn't think about the bag of money not being there; that would be a complete disaster.

On the train ride down, his mind automatically thought of mugging someone in case the money was gone, but the train was too full of theatre and pub crowds going home, and he didn't want to risk it anyway. He would see if the money was there first before doing anything drastic.

So he sat quietly in his moose jumper, an old newspaper covering his crotch, and listened to people's conversations. He almost envied them their normality, and their peaceful, orderly lives. When had his ever been like that?

He thought of his old friend Phil Gator as well. What would he do in Teddy's present situation? Probably take the money and disappear. Gator was so selfish he wouldn't bother trying for revenge any more. He would quit while he was ahead.

Teddy was almost starting to think along the same lines. He was sick of running around the country looking for Jason Campbell, but he wanted to give it one more go. He also hoped the policewoman would still be with him, and taking the two of them out would be the perfect way of ending things. Then he would take the three and a half grand and lie low for a while. He would think about Mr Muscle's offer, but he didn't really want to become a hit man himself. He didn't seem to be very good at it. And if he cocked it up this time with Campbell he would call it a day. It was getting too risky, and it was always something he could do at a later date, maybe if he was driving through Woodvale one day with nothing to do. Knock on Campbell's front door and blow him away. Yes, that sounded like a good idea. He would give it one more go and then quit.

When the train pulled into Redgate it was after ten-thirty and getting cold. Teddy marched quickly out of the station and headed for Woodvale. He had walked the distance once before, the first time he had come to Woodvale, that day he had thrown the brick through Campbell's front window. Although the leggings were riding uncomfortably up his arse, Teddy felt light as he walked, as if he were coming to the end of his journey. Just one more throw of the dice and then have a holiday.

He had to take a slight detour to get to Naughton Road because the direct route passed right in front of the police station. He skipped down a side street and soon he was back to where it had all started. He headed straight for the footpath that was hidden by the hedges, his heart beating faster the closer he got to his bounty.

He found the tree and looked upwards. He couldn't see a thing because it was too dark. So he started climbing, making slow progress. His bandaged hand hurt like hell every time he put pressure on it.

He found the bag exactly where he'd left it and punched the air with relief. He unzipped it quickly and felt inside.

The money was still there and so was the gun. He dropped the bag to the ground and carefully climbed back down.

He pulled back a bit of the hedge and stared across the road at number eight. All the lights were off and he couldn't see the blue Nissan anywhere. That probably meant that Campbell was back on the road, playing his pathetic little songs again, thinking he was in the clear. Teddy couldn't remember where the tour was now, but he still had the piece of paper in his sports bag. He would find a hotel and plan his next move. He stepped away from the hedge and wandered off down the road.

On Tuesday morning Jason woke up in Julie's bed and she turned towards him and said, 'What have you decided?'

'Let's hit the road and get this tour over with,' Jason said. They climbed out of bed and started getting ready.

After yesterday's panic they had decided to sleep on the matter of whether the tour should continue, and Julie had left the decision to Jason. Jason was a believer in sleeping on things, and in the clear light of eight a.m., things didn't seem so bleak. He thought that Teddy Peppers would be a fool to come after him again, and he was confident enough to travel just with Julie by his side, even if she was unarmed. Even though Charing Cross police had forbidden him to tour while Peppers was on the loose, they would now be heading out to East Anglia, so the London police wouldn't know anything about it. And Jason also wanted the four hundred pounds that was there for the taking for four nights of easy work.

So they set off at eleven in the Nissan, heading east on the M25 and crossing through the Dartford tunnel. Then up the M11 and the A11 to Norwich. They arrived just after three, having stopped at a pub for lunch along the way.

It took them a while to find the University of East Anglia, although it wasn't too far from the town centre. Then they turned the car round and headed back to a row of bed and breakfasts they had just passed and checked into one. They stripped off and made love on top of the rock-hard double bed, and then jumped into the bath together. Jason told Julie she was a lot more fun to travel with than Jesse Morgan. She splashed him with soapy water.

When five o'clock rolled around they jumped back into the car and headed for the university. They parked in a large car park and carried Jason's guitars towards the conglomeration of buildings. It took them another fifteen minutes to find the concert hall, as no one seemed to know where it was.

When they walked in, Neil from PMA was already there, his head freshly shaved, and he shook Jason's hand and welcomed him back to the tour. They were shown to his dressing room, a small one with a full-length mirror and a toilet.

After the soundcheck they went to the students' canteen for something to eat, but Jason could feel a lot of nerves going round in his stomach and sensed something was wrong.

'I feel like shit,' he said to Julie. 'Can we go to the bar and get a drink?' He held his right hand in front of him and saw that it was shaking.

When they'd finished eating they went to the students' bar and ordered three glasses of white wine. Jason had two of them. They sat at a small round table and Jason felt very old. The youngsters surrounding them were all around Julie's age, and he thought that maybe she would feel better socializing with them. He put the point to her.

'But I'm with you, you idiot,' she said. 'Live in the present.' She reached over and touched his hand.

'I don't think I want to play tonight,' he said. 'What if Peppers is here somewhere? He's not going to mess around any more. He could shoot me on stage.'

'I thought you'd thought this through already? He's not stupid enough to come back after you. Didn't we agree on that?'

'It seemed like the right decision back in Woodvale. Now I'm not so sure. Can we have another drink?' Jason went to the bar and bought a couple more.

When he came back he said, 'Do you want to hear my "second-best" theory?'

'Your second-best theory. Can't I hear your best theory first?'

'No. This is "second-best" in inverted commas.'

'I'm not with you. You'd better just talk.'

Jason took a sip of wine. 'It's also the "support act" theory.'

'Now you're really confusing me.'

'OK. A support act goes on tour with someone, and nobody pays to see them, they're all there to see the main act. If the support act is lousy it makes the main act look better; if the support act is good it just warms up the audience for the main act. The main act can't lose; the support act always loses.'

'Easy to understand so far.'

'Therefore, being a support act all the time is bound to grind you down, because you always see yourself as second-best. Even though it's good experience for a while, in the long run you can't win. And that's really quite a good metaphor for life.'

'How do you mean?'

'We can't waste our lives being the support act all the time. We have to go for the big one, try to become the main act. I've now realized why most of the time I've felt bad about performing. I've always been the support act. I've never been top of the bill. So the decision I have to make is, either get myself a manager and go for top billing, or give it up and concentrate on teaching. When I'm teaching I feel a lot better about myself because I'm the main act, I'm top of the bill.'

'It could apply to me as well,' Julie said.

'It does. You're in a male-dominated world and they like

to keep you in your place. They don't like the fact that you can shoot better than any of them, and so taking your gun away is great for them. The answer to all their problems. Putting you in your place. Keeping you the support act. You have to decide whether you can carry on in such an environment.'

'What a pair we make.'

'Different worlds, similar situations.'

'So the thing to do is to get my authorized-shot status back?'

'Yeah. And then really piss them off by getting some exams and rising up the ranks. Get to the top of the pile.'

Julie nodded. 'So what are you going to do?'

'I'm still thinking about it, but I think my support days are over. I have to decide whether to strike out on my own. Playing music live can be very unsettling, though. You get the highs after a good gig, but then get very depressed after the bad ones or if things aren't progressing. That's why pop stars drink and take drugs so much. Their emotions are subjected to a roller-coaster ride. Adoration and then the abyss. How about you?'

'I'll have to think about it. But I won't let them beat me easily.'

Jason felt a little better after his speech, but still didn't want to get up on stage. It was a similar feeling to that first night in Glasgow when he'd received Peppers's note. Maybe slightly worse. He would just have to try to get through it. Sing the songs he knew best and don't do anything fancy. Maybe he was having a delayed reaction of some kind.

They went back to the dressing room and he tuned up his Martin, while Julie sat on a chair watching. At five to eight Neil knocked on the door and Jason went to wait in the corridor. Julie kissed him for luck and Jason was left with his thoughts, the worst five minutes of any performing day. And things didn't get much better when he walked on stage.

The concert hall was more like a large bar: circular tables

with chairs, a raised section around one side and at the back. There were only two hundred and fifty in the audience, but that didn't make things much easier. Even with Julie patrolling among them.

Jason launched into his first song, 'Too Far, Too Soon', and his voice was all over the place, shaking and flat on far too many notes. He tried to talk his way through the song more, a technique he had learned over the years, and that seemed to work better. As there was no power in his voice he dropped his capo down a fret for the next song and continued with the talking voice. No one seemed to notice.

As he performed he couldn't help but scan the hall for bald-headed men, but there seemed so many these days it was a hopeless task. He kept his talking in between songs to a bare minimum and left the stage after half an hour to muted applause. He was grateful just to get back to the dressing room alive.

Julie came in with two large glasses of wine and gave him a big hug.

'I can't go on with this,' Jason said. 'I feel like a total wreck. I think the strain is beginning to tell.'

'You didn't sound too bad,' she said. 'Just a little wobbly.'

'Wobbly?' He managed to smile. 'Now there's a new description.'

Julie pinched his cheek. 'Let's pack up and leave. What you need is a good massage and an early night. We can decide what to do tomorrow.'

'That's what we said last night.'

They packed up and went back to the bed and breakfast.

33

Wednesday morning was Jesse Morgan's day of release, and Nicola had driven from Woodvale to pick him up. As a way of thanking her, and to celebrate his early retirement, he was going to treat her to a few days in Cambridge. He had already booked two tickets for that night's Calista Shaw show, and he was looking forward to seeing Jason again. That's if Jason recognised him with his bald head.

Ian Kiddie had rung him last night and given him the details about Teddy Peppers' miraculous escape. Morgan couldn't believe such a thing could happen, and was glad he didn't have to go back to work; if it wasn't the judges letting criminals back on the streets, it was the security vans. What was the point in working any more? He would have a few months' rest and then find an easier job with regular hours and no responsibility.

He hobbled out of hospital with a walking stick and climbed into Nicola's car. It was an unusually sunny day for October, and they talked about the implications of Peppers' escape as Nicola drove.

'Does that mean Jason's in danger again?' she asked.

'I really don't know,' Morgan said. 'He's got Julie Beech with him, but she doesn't have a gun. I'll be there tonight, of course. I've got my trusty walking stick.'

Nicola gave him a disapproving look. 'You're not going to get involved in anything. You've done more than enough already.'

Morgan looked out of the window. He felt he hadn't done a thing yet, just got himself shot three times. He wasn't going to tell Nicola his real reason for going to Cambridge. He was going because he was sure Teddy Peppers would be there.

After reading more of the Joseph Campbell book he was convinced that Peppers would 'follow his bliss'. Being a criminal was what made Peppers happy, and he wasn't about to change overnight, even though his escape had offered him a miraculous second chance. Peppers would pursue Jason until he was dead; Morgan was ninety-nine per cent sure of that.

As the countryside sped by he thought about his non-drinking tally as well. With the time in hospital knocking him out for a week, he now hadn't had a drink for over three weeks. He felt more clear-headed than he'd ever been, even with all the drugs they'd pumped into him. He looked at Nicola and said, 'We'll see.'

She shook her head.

The concert that night was meant to be at the Corn Exchange, but when Jason and Julie walked in at midday they found Neil in a bad mood, talking on his mobile in the foyer. When he'd finished he walked over to them and said, 'The concert might be off.'

After his problems the night before, Jason tried hard not to look relieved. He had woken up this morning just wanting to go home, but had decided to be professional and finish the tour. 'What do you mean?' he asked.

'Calista Shaw is feeling the strain apparently, and may even cancel the rest of the tour.'

'What's wrong with her?' Julie asked.

'She had a bad night in Norwich. She forgot a few words here and there and even started giggling during one song. She says the tour's caught up with her. Too many dates. Now I have to wait for another phone call to tell me for definite. I'm afraid we'll just have to hang around awhile and see what happens.'

'Well, there are worse places to hang around,' Julie said. 'Let's go and walk the streets.'

Neil nodded, and the three of them left the building.

They walked around for a couple of hours, past the different colleges, looking in shops and buying cups of coffee. Jason hoped the tour would be cancelled so he could go back home. He had decided he wasn't going to be a support act any more, and was going to pack in live performing altogether. He'd had a good run at it, and didn't have the energy or heart to take it any further. He was over forty, and it was time to make his own decisions in life, do the things he wanted to do. No more compromises.

The other major decision he had come to was that he was going to put his house on the market and put his past with Heather behind him once and for all. He thought the house was jinxed, judging by all that had happened in the last two years. He could buy a small flat in Woodvale and get rid of his massive mortgage and the burden of being a landlord. As for his collection of guitars, he would just have to sell a lot of them, but that would be a small price to pay. He didn't play most of them anyway, and it was high time he trimmed down his life to a more manageable scale.

As for his relationship with Julie, he would just play it week by week and see what happened. Things seemed to be going fine for the moment, and that was good enough. He had told her his decisions on the drive to Cambridge, and she had been pleased. She said she was having major thoughts about her career too. It seemed as though everything was about to change.

Jason felt good walking along the streets of Cambridge holding Julie's hand. It was a fine town to be in, and she was a fine-looking woman. He liked the architecture of the colleges, the students on their bicycles and the narrow River Cam which they walked over several times. They watched people going lazily up the river in punts, and it looked a fun thing to do.

Neil paused now and then to ring his head office in Liverpool, but there was still no news about Calista Shaw's decision. They went back to the Corn Exchange to see if they'd heard anything, but just got blank looks from the soundmen. Neil was seething. Jason was feeling better by the minute.

'Let's go to the river and hire a punt,' Julie suggested.

'Sounds like a good idea to me,' Neil said.

So they walked back on to the street.

Teddy Peppers watched them leave from a doorway opposite the Corn Exchange. He had been in Cambridge an hour or so and was wearing his normal clothes again, with a baseball cap to cover his baldness. He couldn't believe his luck when he saw the broken-nosed policewoman with Campbell. He knew he had made the right decision, coming after them one more time.

He stepped out of the doorway and followed along behind, carrying his sports bag. They were chatting happily among themselves, oblivious to any danger lurking behind, and he detested them for their complacency. There was another bald bloke with them, Teddy recognizing him as the man who'd given him a refund in Portsmouth. He would be an extra problem, but if he had to kill the three of them, then so be it. He was getting excited at the prospect of more action. And Cambridge just added to the atmosphere. He felt like he was in one of those stupid Morse programmes. But this was a different town, and the story would have a different outcome.

Jesse Morgan and Nicola arrived in Cambridge around three o'clock. They parked and walked to the Corn Exchange to pick up their tickets and to see if Jason and Julie were around. They found a waitress in the foyer cleaning tables and asked if she'd seen them. She didn't know who they were talking about until Morgan described them.

'I know who you mean,' the waitress said. 'Yes, they left a few minutes ago. With a bald man.'

Morgan felt panic grip his stomach. 'A bald man? Are you sure?'

'Yes, quite sure. I think they've gone to the river to hire a punt.'

'Which way is that?'

'Turn left out of here, then left again. It's not too far.'

Before Nicola could say anything Morgan was heading out of the door with his walking stick. She ran after him and grabbed his arm. 'What's the big panic?' she asked, a worried look on her face.

'Teddy Peppers is now bald, if you remember.'

Morgan was imagining Jason and Julie being marched to the river to be shot. He cursed his painful leg and tried to walk faster.

Jason paid for a punt at the Scudamore boathouse, which was next to a nice-looking pub called The Anchor. He fancied going in there later for a few drinks.

Neil offered to do all the hard work, so Jason and Julie sat down on the seats and took the piss out of him while he struggled with the pole. Eventually he got the hang of it, and they made slow progress along the water.

There weren't many other punts on the river, and they waved to tourists who strolled along the banks. The sun was still out and it was almost summer weather. Jason thought it a perfect setting for an end-of-tour party, and hoped that would be the message when Neil's mobile eventually rang. He glanced behind Neil and saw a man in a blue baseball cap, carrying a sports bag, climbing into another punt.

Morgan and Nicola reached the boathouse out of breath. Morgan flashed his ID at the young man and said he needed a punt, pronto. The man led them to one, and pointed to where the last few boats had gone. Morgan told Nicola to stay behind.

'I don't want you along,' he said. 'Just in case things get hairy. Can you call the police and tell them where we are?'

Nicola looked at Morgan's bald head and said, 'You think things will get hairy?'

Morgan smiled, climbed on board and pushed away from the bank.

As he reached the middle of the river he thought he could see a few boats in the distance, and after a few pushes on the pole soon got the hang of this archaic mode of transport. Then he was moving across the water comfortably, making good ground on the boats up ahead. If he couldn't run because of his leg, at least he could push a punt as quickly as the next man. He just hoped he still had enough strength in his arms for what might happen after that.

The mobile attached to Neil's waist rang. He stopped pushing on the pole and leaned it against the side of the punt. He took the phone off his waist and spoke into it. 'Where am I now?' he said after a few moments. 'I'm going down the River Cam in a punt. With Jason Campbell.'

Jason saw the absurdity of it and laughed. He listened to Neil's fragmented conversation, and then started looking back down the river. He could see the man in the blue baseball cap heading towards them, although his punt was zigzagging all over the place. And behind him there was another punt, this one with a bald man pushing it along, a bald man with a goatee beard. Jason was getting sick of all these slapheads. Why did they have to shave themselves? Wasn't there plenty of time for baldness when they were old?

Neil finished his conversation and said, 'The tour's off. She's cancelled the whole lot.'

Jason was relieved. He stood up and thrust his arms into the air.

*

Jesse Morgan passed another punter, a man in a baseball cap who was having trouble with his boat, sending it in all directions, cursing out loud.

Morgan saw Jason's punt about ten yards away with the bald Teddy Peppers standing at the back of it. He pushed harder on his pole and saw a black object in Peppers's hand that he was pointing at Jason. Morgan really started panicking when Jason stood up and held his arms in the air. He gave one final shove on the pole, then lifted it out of the water and pointed it at Peppers like a jousting knight of old. It struck Peppers hard in the back and he toppled off the punt and into the water.

Morgan brought his punt to a stop, and for some reason Jason was saying to him, 'What the fuck did you do that for?'

They looked at each other across the water. The man looked familiar to Jason, but Julie got it first.

'Hello, Inspector Morgan,' she said. 'What brings you to Cambridge?'

'Is that you, Jesse?' Jason said. 'Where's all your hair?'

'Shaved it off,' Morgan said. 'I think I just made a big mistake.'

'Well, everyone seems to be doing it these days,' Jason said.

'No, I meant him,' Morgan said, pointing to Neil who was paddling around in the water. 'Sorry Neil,' he said. 'I thought you were Teddy Peppers.'

'Well, you owe me a mobile phone,' Neil said, dropping his wet one into the punt.

'Is Teddy Peppers meant to be here?' Jason asked.

Morgan shrugged. 'They told me at the hall that you'd gone to the river with a bald man. I presumed it was Peppers. I forgot about Neil being bald.'

But Jason was only half listening. He was being distracted by the man in the punt coming up behind Morgan, a man with a big bandage on his right hand. It looked as though there might be a collision.

Then the man took off his baseball cap and threw it into the punt in a rage, and the alarm bells went off in Jason's head. As the man reached for something in the boat Jason pointed and said, 'I think he's right behind you.'

Like most people, Teddy Peppers had never been in a punt in his life. He kept digging the pole into the water but couldn't get the boat to go straight. It was even harder with his sore hand. He found the whole thing totally frustrating. What a stupid fucking way of getting around. Stupid transport for upper-class twits. He had already been passed by another bald man, and now that man had pulled up alongside Campbell's punt and someone had fallen in. There were too many people getting in the way. It was all getting out of hand! He was so angry he pulled off his baseball cap and threw it into the boat. It was only then that he realized he'd made a mistake and exposed his bald head. He scrambled for the sports bag and the Beretta.

Morgan saw the fear on Jason's face. He was still holding the pole horizontally, and when he turned, it whacked into the bald man who had sneaked up behind him. The man fell off the punt and into the water, and Morgan dived in after him.

He caught Teddy Peppers as he was coming up for air, recognizing the man who'd shot him now; about the same build as Neil but a lot scarier-looking with no hair. He grabbed him by the throat and pushed him under the water, but Peppers was strong and managed to surface again. Peppers lashed out with his left arm and smacked Morgan on the chin, but then Neil appeared from nowhere and got Peppers around the throat. Between the two of them they managed to push Peppers down again, but he still managed to force himself up.

Morgan was preparing for another assault when a punt

pole flashed through the air like a javelin and hit Peppers on the side of the head with a thud. The blow raised blood and Morgan took his chance. He jumped on top of him and held him under again, and this time Peppers didn't struggle. When he knew he was dead, he let go of the body and pulled it to the surface.

He looked up at the other punt, trying to catch his breath.

'Nice throw,' he said. 'Who was it?'

He expected Julie Beech to raise her hand, but in fact it was Jason.

'How does it feel to have your first hit?' Morgan said.

Jason looked down at the three bald men in the water, two of them alive, one of them dead, their heads glistening in the sun. He was glad it was all over, and surprised that he had been able to throw a punt pole so accurately.

Julie came to his side and hugged him. Then he sat down in the punt and took off his cowboys boots. Ever since he'd bought them they'd caused him nothing but trouble. He stood up and threw them into the River Cam.

34

Five weeks later, Jesse Morgan held his official leaving party in The Red Lion pub. Jason had been pleased to get an invite, but was going on his own because Julie was working.

He walked to the pub so he could drink what he wanted, and when he arrived it was already crowded. He had never seen so many crew-cuts in one place, and searched for Morgan. He eventually saw him in a corner, surrounded by other cops, one of them the ginger-haired one Jason had met once before.

While he was getting a glass of wine at the bar, the policeman called Garnett came over, the one that Teddy Peppers had stabbed at Jason's house. They shook hands and Jason asked how he was.

'On the mend,' Garnett said. 'It takes more than a flick knife to penetrate this lot.' He squeezed his stomach proudly. 'And on the subject of penetration,' he continued, 'I heard that you and Beech were more than just close friends.' He laughed, and Jason wondered if he could get away with a quick pinch on his stomach wound. He chose to ignore the question instead.

'You know, you're the envy of the whole station,' Garnett said. 'You're the first one to get her in the sack that we know of.'

Jason winced. He had to get away from the man.

He pushed himself from the bar and walked over to Morgan's table. Jesse's hair was growing back quickly, although it looked a little greyer than before. He smiled at Jason and stood to shake hands.

'Hey there, superstar,' he said, and told the other coppers to make room.

Jason sat down next to the big man, and felt proud to be sitting there. 'I saw you in the papers,' he said. 'A real tour de force.'

Morgan laughed. 'The money will come in handy.'

'How much did they pay you?'

'Twenty thousand,' Morgan said. 'A nice way to start retirement.'

Jason shook his head in disbelief. A Japanese tourist had videoed Morgan's fight with Peppers from the banks of the River Cam, and segments of it had been shown that night on the late news. There had been over a hundred calls of complaint afterwards, and then the newspapers had got interested. Morgan had sold his story to the *Sunday Mirror*, and it had run for two weeks under the headline 'Tour de Force.'

'I'm surprised the police let you sell it,' Jason said.

'They wouldn't normally. But as I'm retiring they didn't mind.'

'You got lucky there.'

'I did indeed. But I hear you've had some luck as well.'

Jason smiled. In the weeks since Teddy Peppers's death, he had had three record companies on the phone wanting to sign him up. He too had been on the TV news clip, and his name had also featured heavily in Morgan's article. It seemed that now the record companies had an angle with which to sell a CD, they were flocking round him. Jason had hastily rethought about quitting performing, and had travelled into London to see Charles Penn. Penn was now his manager, and was in negotiation with them all.

'They're not massive offers,' Jason said. 'The one we like best is from Pilgrim Records. A rootsy outfit. I get ten thousand up front, and they'll give me a budget to make my first album.'

'That's great. I'll buy a copy.'

'But we're also trying for a publishing deal as well. That's where the really big money is. If I can get a big star or two to record some of my songs, I'll be rolling in it.'

'I wish you luck. You'll be following your bliss. Have you ever heard of that saying?'

'Wasn't it Joseph Campbell?'

A look of surprise came to Morgan's face. 'How did you know that?'

'I do read the occasional book, you know. It's a good saying, but I can't say I've paid it a lot of attention.'

'You should. I'll lend you a book if you like.'

'OK. That would be good.'

Jason watched Morgan take a sip of his soft drink. He wondered if he should cut down his drinking now as well. He would soon be a busy man, and drinking would only get in the way. Charles Penn was also lining him up for another tour, another support slot, this time with Gillian Welch. It would be different being a support act this time, though, because he would have something to promote and could also travel by car. His days of touting for free accommodation from the stage were over.

'Did you hear about Calista Shaw?' Morgan asked. 'She's just had a nervous breakdown. I read about it in one of the country magazines. Apparently she's had enough of touring and is going to take a year off.'

'It's just as well she didn't know what was going on with us, then. That would've finished her off for good.'

Morgan nodded. 'We never did get to know her, did we?'

Jason shook his head. 'If I ever get to be a star, I'll make sure I mix with the support.'

'Yeah. What you don't experience positively, you'll experience negatively.'

Jason laughed. 'Joseph Campbell again?'

Jason left at closing time feeling pretty drunk. He had bought some drinks for the others and had listened to some pretty hilarious police stories. He would keep in touch with Morgan and invite him to some future shows.

As he wandered down the road, he thought how life couldn't get much better at the moment. He had put his house on the market and already had one offer; he was on the verge of signing a record deal, and, best of all, things were still going well with Julie. She had decided to stay on in the force, and it looked as though she would soon get her authorized-shot status back. Maybe sometime down the line they could think about living together, although Jason was still worried a little about the age difference between them. He was going to buy a smaller house so he could still play all his instruments loud, and then they could make their future plans at their own pace.

He heard a police siren behind him then, and a car approaching at speed. He expected it to rush past, but instead it slowed down and pulled up next to him. The passenger window wound down and Julie was sitting there.

'Excuse me, sir,' she said, 'but don't you think you've had a little too much to drink?'

Jason shook his head. 'On the contrary, officer. I don't think I've had enough.'

Julie smiled, turned around in her seat and opened the back door. 'Get in,' she said.

Standing on the pavement at closing time, waiting for Nicola to appear so he could drive her home, Jesse Morgan felt incredibly at peace with the world. Now that the last formalities of his police career were over, he felt that tomorrow would be the first day of the rest of his life, to use a well-worn cliché.

For the last month while he'd been recuperating he had felt the tension draining out of his body almost day by day. It was goodbye to the years of shift work, the years of making instant stressful decisions that could change people's lives, and most of all the monotony of the paperwork. From now on, he would be making all the rules by which he lived, and he was looking forward to every single sober minute of it.

The pub door opened behind him and Nicola walked out. She shivered in the cold and walked over to him. In the past few weeks they had talked about their relationship and had agreed to give it another go. They were sleeping together again, and for some reason it seemed more erotic this time round.

'Where's the car?' she asked.

'Just down the road. There were so many people here I couldn't find a place to park.'

'You're a popular man, Jesse Morgan. How will you survive without them?'

'I'll just have to make do with you,' he said.

She kissed him on the lips and stroked his beard. 'You should keep your goatee. It makes you look hip.'

Morgan laughed. He had never been called hip in his life before. Maybe this could be his new image. He took Nicola's arm and they walked off down the road. She smiled up at him and said, 'I'm glad you're not a slaphead any more.'